QUANTUM PERIL

Nolan Lee

This is a work of fiction. Names, characters, places, and incidents are either the product of the author's imagination or are used fictitiously, and any resemblance to actual persons (living or dead), businesses, events, or locales is entirely coincidental.

Graphics in this book were created by the author with OpenAI DALL-E and Adobe Photoshop.

QUANTUM PERIL

Published by N. Lee Publications

Hardcover ISBN 979-8-9907997-0-7
Paperback ISBN 979-8-9907997-1-4

Our books may be purchased in bulk for promotional, educational, or business use. Please contact your local bookseller or N. Lee Publications at AuthorNolanLee@gmail.com.

Follow Nolan Lee for book announcements and exclusive content!
Instagram: @AuthorNolanLee

First Edition

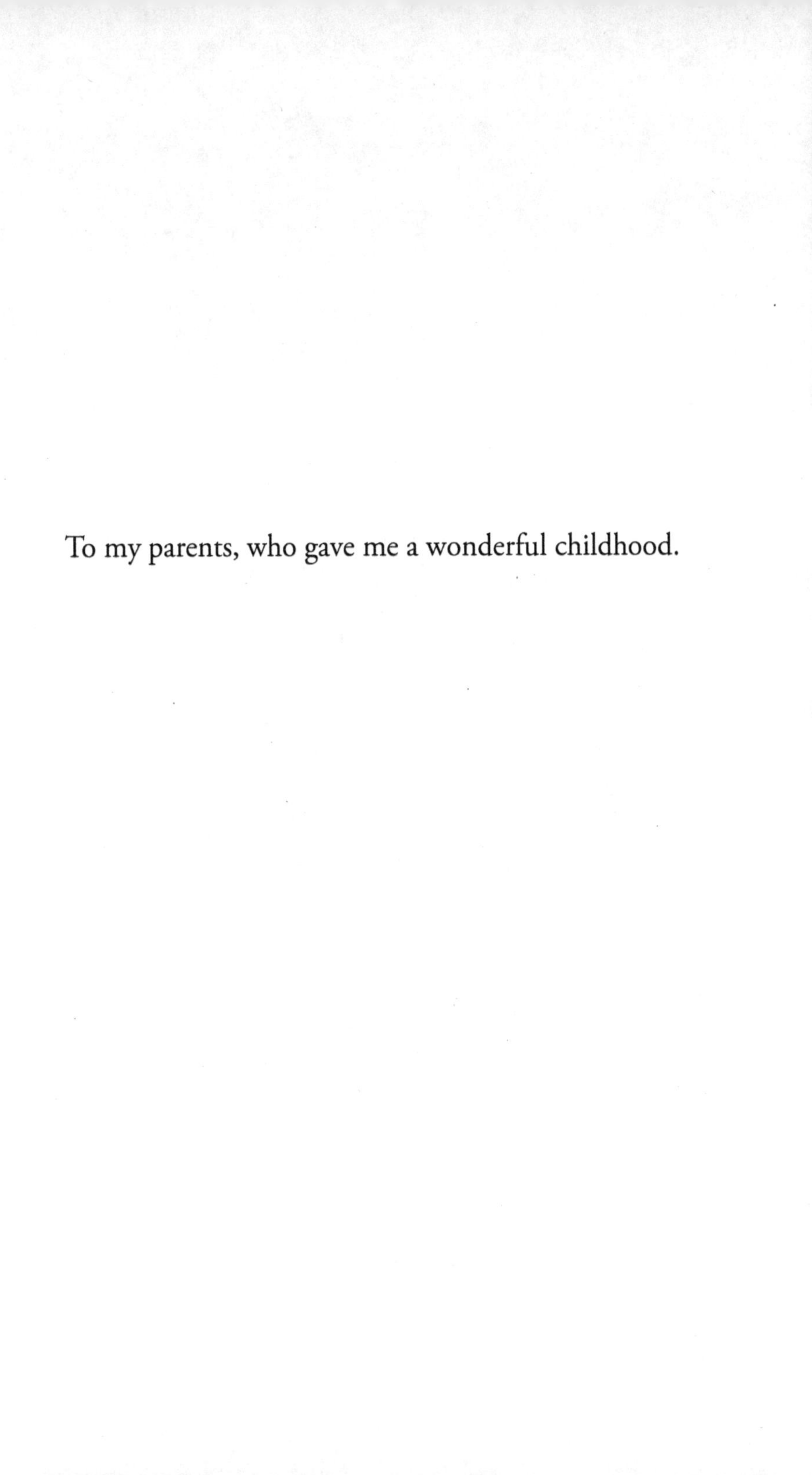

To my parents, who gave me a wonderful childhood.

"This is the most important, most competitive, and most dangerous relationship that the United States has in the world right now and will, I think, for the next decade or so."

Nicholas Burns, US Ambassador to China

"The people of China must fight against those domestic and foreign forces and elements that are hostile to and undermine our country's socialist system."

Constitution of the People's Republic of China

"USCYBERCOM plans, coordinates, integrates, synchronizes and conducts activities to: direct the operations and defense of specified Department of Defense information networks and; prepare to, and when directed, conduct full spectrum military cyberspace operations in order to enable actions in all domains, ensure US/Allied freedom of action in cyberspace and deny the same to our adversaries."

United States Cyber Command

"Very many members of our family have given their lives, killed by the Kuomintang and the American imperialists."

Mao Zedong, Founder of the People's Republic of China

"Let your plans be dark and impenetrable as night, and when you move, fall like a thunderbolt."

Sun Tzu, The Art of War

Prologue

July 4, 2058

The man flipped down the visor for his MetaMind headset. The weight of this meeting pressed down on him. He wondered what could happen if he made a mistake.

His visor filled with a detailed, immersive landscape—a grassy field, a virtual sky painted with hues of orange and pink, and a forest of trees surrounding the area.

"Welcome, Titanium Dragon!" spoke the game announcer's voice. "Medieval Swords" was a popular MetaMind game amongst teens, but it was also one of the few games which supported post-quantum encryption. The game session was secured end-to-end against snooping.

He could feel the cool breeze on his face and smelled a faint scent of lilacs. It wasn't just a visual or auditory experience; it was almost real—all thanks to his MetaMind's ventilation and artificial olfactory systems. In his left hand, he gripped a metal shield, and in his right, the hilt of a long double-edged sword. He felt like a knight in 16th-century Europe.

An opponent materialized, the sunlight reflecting off his stainless steel armor. The mask bore the face of a skull —a shimmering visage of intimidation. After a few fierce exchanges and clanging of steel, the opponent dropped his weapons.

"Let's talk business," the knight spoke. His voice was modulated by an anonymizer. He sounded like an alien speaking an octave too low.

"Golden Rat, I presume?" asked Titanium Dragon, also modulating his voice with an anonymizer.

"Payment?" inquired Golden Rat. A crypto wallet address showed up in the chat. Titanium Dragon copied it into his crypto program and sent 500,000 FedCoins. "This better be worth it," he thought.

"Do you know about the 2020 Pandemic?" Golden Rat asked. Titanium nodded, remembering his father's stories from the era. But that was almost 40 years ago; the world had moved on.

"The problem you are trying to solve started with the Pandemic," Golden Rat continued.

"That was almost 40 years ago. What do you mean?" Titanium asked, intrigued.

Golden Rat continued. "The Pandemic reshaped the global economy. Governments shut down major parts of the economy for years and central banks printed trillions of dollars to backstop paper losses. The West atrophied, and this gave China a rare opportunity to catch up. China was the only global power in 2020 to experience positive GDP growth. Scale this out over decades and you understand why China achieved quantum computing before the United States. It's why they eventually surpassed the US in military spending and GDP. The Pandemic was the inflection point—the decline of the West, and the rise of the People's Republic of China."

"I didn't come here for a history lesson about Communist China," Titanium replied. "Do you have anything actionable?"

Golden Rat continued. "They are on the brink of something monumental. It could be the final checkmate on not only the West, but the whole world. The Chinese Communist Party is trying to make their global power permanent. The breadcrumbs I've found through my network all point to a location."

"What did you find?" Asked Titanium Dragon.

"Check out these coordinates: 21.451115, 111.314543."

Titanium punched the coordinates into his map tool. "This looks like an ordinary bay for commercial ships."

Golden Rat nodded. "It's rarely used these days because there are better ports nearby. However, there is unusual activity: frequent supply shipments, and military checkpoints coming and going. That's all I know."

Titanium pondered the information as Golden Rat's avatar dissolved into nothingness. A message notification blinked in his visor's corner—an end-to-end encrypted message: "We're running out of time."

Pulling off his MetaMind headset, Titanium Dragon pondered the information. His heart raced. The quest for the truth had just become even more perilous. But there was no turning back now, not when he was so close to the answers.

Lat: 21.451115, Long: 111.314543

Part One

Quantum Warrior

1

San Francisco, California (four months earlier)

Perched at his apartment window, Marvin Wong surveyed the bustling tapestry of Japantown. Below, cherry blossoms painted the air with their delicate hues, as shoppers meandered past vibrant shops. This oasis of serenity was a stark contrast to the rest of San Francisco, a city grappling with the tentacles of chaos. Japantown's unique tranquility was a testament to the community's resolve, safeguarded by the vigilant presence of heavily armed private security and stringent identification checkpoints.

Marvin's residence here came at a steep price, the cost of maintaining bulletproof windows and 24/7 security patrols were part of his monthly rent. Yet, as he gazed upon the scene, he knew it was worth every penny. Step beyond the confines of this sanctuary, and the city's harsh reality awaited: a labyrinth of drugs, illicit fencing operations, and the haunts of hardened criminals. Japantown was more than just his home; it was a fortress of peace amidst an urban battlefield.

As Marvin's gaze drifted beyond the colorful facades and serene parks of Japantown, he could see the stark contrast in the adjacent neighborhoods. Blocks upon blocks of derelict buildings, their once vibrant colors faded to a monochrome palette of grays and browns, told the story of a city besieged by neglect. The streets were littered with debris, the remnants of failed businesses and abandoned homes. In these parts of the city, the air was thick with pollution and despair.

Self-driving shuttles whirred along the city's transit arteries, and for a toll, one could drive on these elevated electrified highways and avoid the anarchy below. Engineered for resilience, most vehicles in San Francisco boasted bulletproof glass and inch-thick ballistic armor—a necessary shield against the flying rocks, bricks, and stray bullets that characterized the lawless expanses of the city.

The self-driving cars seemed out of place amidst the slums of San Francisco, like a glimpse of a future that never fully arrived. The sleek forms of flying police drones occasionally swept overhead, their cameras scanning the streets below. Though they demonstrated the city's advanced surveillance capabilities, their necessity was a reminder of the city's tragic decline. San Francisco suffered under suffocating regulations and corruption.

Marvin turned away from the window, a heavy sigh escaping him. The contrast between his neighborhood and the rest of San Francisco was a daily reminder of the city's potential, squandered by decades of neglect and mismanagement. As he logged in to his MetaMind, he contemplated the contradictions in his life. Despite the technological wonders at their fingertips, he lived in a suffocating reality, where progress was measured not by advancements in quality of life, but by the ability to survive another day.

Marvin's job as a software engineer for a prominent AI cybersecurity firm provided a reliable paycheck but did little to challenge his innate skills. He lived a decent life —he could afford a one-bedroom apartment, good food, and two vacations per year. But sometimes, he wondered if there was more to life than the corporate grind.

Every so often, when the monotony became too much, Marvin would indulge in his secret passion: hacking. Not the dangerous, headline-making sort. No, Marvin's hacks were subtler white-collar hacks that were more mischievous than malevolent.

On slow days, Marvin would stroll down to the local library. He wouldn't go to read but rather to tweak the system, extending due dates on his borrowed material or submitting purchase orders for expensive datasets he wanted the library to carry. A vending machine in his building would mysteriously malfunction once in a while, granting Marvin a free packet of chips or a soda. These exploits gave him a sense of accomplishment that his job could never offer. He was virtually invisible, just another face in the bustling crowd, but secretly wielding power over these small computer systems.

His roots traced back to a Chinese family that had made Los Angeles their home in the 1920s. He often recalled the tales of his ancestors' resilience, grit, and determination to thrive in a new land. They took whatever they could carry and abandoned China as the Red Army marched south towards Guangdong. Refugees from the Chinese Civil War, Marvin's family started from nothing in Los Angeles. Many of the men in his family enlisted to fight for the United States in WWII. Uncle Sam made a deal with immigrants; if you survived the war, you could apply for citizenship.

These stories were passed down like heirlooms, inspiring Marvin to venture out and carve his own path. Four years at Caltech yielded a coveted degree in computer science, and he easily landed a job at the top cybersecurity firm in San Francisco. He also hoped that, one day, he could give back to the country that had given his family so much.

2

In the treacherous corporate waters of Silicon Valley, Marvin Wong navigated with the caution of a seasoned sailor. His manager's sudden meeting invite, devoid of agenda, sent a ripple of unease through him. Spontaneous manager meetings without an agenda typically had two outcomes for your career: promotion or termination.

Marvin's manager materialized on the kitchen counter as a hologram, its flickering form a ghostly apparition in the mundane setting of his home. "Marvin, you're a fantastic engineer," the hologram declared, the voice devoid of the warmth that once accompanied human praise. "But currently, you're not performing at the level we expect here at CyberBricks."

The holographic image gave his manager a semblance of presence, despite the fact that Marvin had never met him in person. Sometimes, Marvin wondered whether his manager was a real person at all or just another AI-powered management program designed to monitor and evaluate employees more efficiently.

"I'm not sure what you're talking about," Marvin retorted, his tone mixing confusion with a tinge of irritation. "I've delivered on every task, often shipping code far in advance of deadlines. I wrote 10% of the source code in one of our most profitable products."

"Yes, but after you deliver on your assigned tasks, you don't seek out other work. You just wait until the next task is assigned. We want you to show initiative and proactively find more work to do," the hologram continued, its voice devoid of emotion. "Here at CyberBricks we want everyone to feel excited to work every day."

Silicon Valley had lost its way. After the MBAs and AI algorithms usurped every management role, most companies transitioned from a results-oriented model to an incessant grind. Companies wanted both quality *and* quantity; they wanted to squeeze every drop of utility out of an employee's workweek. It was common for managers to add scope to employee roles without a commensurate pay increase. And every quarter, managers placed the bottom 10% on notice for firing regardless of actual performance. It was the new normal in the corporate world.

"We've got to put you on a Performance Improvement Plan," the hologram announced, using the euphemistic term that sent a chill down Marvin's spine. "Our Human Resources team will reach out to you with more details. That is all."

As the hologram faded away, Marvin cursed under his breath. "Not a damn PIP," he muttered. In Silicon Valley, being placed on a PIP was widely regarded as the kiss of death for any employment contract. It was the beginning of the end. It meant that the employer was creating a paper trail to record (or fabricate) evidence of laziness or misconduct, thus building an ironclad legal case to justify firing you. While California remained an employee-friendly state even in 2058, PIPs allowed employers to bypass many of the legal hurdles associated with termination.

Marvin wasn't particularly passionate about his job at the cybersecurity firm. The majority of his co-workers were junior engineers who relied heavily on AI assistance to write any usable code. Marvin, on the other hand, was one of the few remaining engineers who could still craft code from scratch, and he did it faster than most. Ironically, his efficiency was now being punished; he was labeled "lazy" for not taking on more projects even though the projects he completed were high impact. But for Marvin, a job was just a means to an end. He wanted to complete his tasks early, receive his paycheck, and enjoy the rest of his life outside the confines of endless coding.

But now, with this PIP looming over him, Marvin felt a knot tighten in his stomach. Unemployment in California had risen to 30%, and welfare checks weren't enough to support a life in San Francisco. As he sat back in his desk chair, Marvin put on his MetaMind to browse job listings, his mind racing with the possibilities of escape.

As Marvin focused on his work, a message notification from HR popped up. He clicked into it and viewed the terms of his PIP. It detailed numerous additional objectives he was expected to meet, none of which seemed relevant to his current projects. It was clear they were setting him up to fail, creating impossible conditions to justify his eventual dismissal. Frustration welled up inside him as he read through the unreasonable demands, each one a reminder of how impersonal and cruel CyberBricks had become.

The cybersecurity firm was once a vibrant start-up praised for its innovative approach and groundbreaking technology. As it grew, it was swallowed by the corporate ethos that prioritized profits over innovation and employee satisfaction. Marvin remembered the early days, the excitement and camaraderie that came with working on something meaningful. Now, those days felt like a distant memory, overshadowed by the relentless pressure to perform and the looming threat of replacement by either a younger, cheaper engineer or an artificial intelligence program.

"Maybe I just need to find something more interesting," Marvin thought. "I never liked this job anyway."

3

Marvin was slim and stood with a slightly hunched posture—thanks to all the time spent coding on MetaMind or staring at computer displays. Standing 5’11” and weighing about 160 pounds, the 30 year-old engineer was not someone you’d send into a fist fight. But what he lacked in brawn, he made up in coding skills. And today, he was coding.

He looked at different virtual computer screens projected around his room through his MetaMind headset. MetaMind represented the cutting edge in augmented reality; it allowed you to play photorealistic video games, watch movies, or write code on virtual monitors without causing motion sickness or eye strain.

Marvin opened up his MetaMail application. His inbox was inundated with junk mail, but one advertisement caught his eye. It was an advertisement from the US Navy. Curiosity piqued, he tapped on the ad. His MetaMind projected a vivid holographic video in front of him. The display was impressive: a dynamic montage of cyber operatives in action, the American flag waving proudly in the digital wind.

The narration kicked in, powerful and resonant, "In an era where cyber threats loom large over our nation's security, the United States Fleet Cyber Command is calling on America's most talented cybersecurity experts to step forward." The imagery shifted to scenes of intense cyber training exercises and high-tech warfare simulations.

"Marvin, are you the one we're looking for?" the voice said (MetaMind ads often used generative AI to address users by name).

The voice continued, "We are currently offering direct commissions to qualified civilian cybersecurity professionals. Join us and be directly commissioned as a second lieutenant, after completing a rigorous officer bootcamp. Your skills can safeguard our national security and you can continue your career on the cutting edge of cybersecurity. Would you like to learn more?"

"Sure, tell me," Marvin replied. The ad continued.

Marvin watched, intrigued, as the video detailed the perks of joining, including advanced cyber warfare training, a competitive salary, and the honor of serving the country at a critical time. "Protect our country from cyber threats—be the tip of the spear!" the advertisement read.

As the ad concluded, he received a follow-up MetaMail with instructions to apply to the program. Marvin felt a spark of excitement—a refreshing contrast to the dull frustration he had been feeling. The thought of applying his skills in such a high-stakes environment, and actually making a difference on a national level, was curiously appealing.

He sat back and removed his headset, his mind racing. This could be the escape he was looking for! It offered a chance to break free from the corporate grind and dive into something truly impactful. With his background and expertise, he was a prime candidate, and the idea of serving as a second lieutenant in US Fleet Cyber Command excited him. Marvin knew that this opportunity would not only change his career trajectory, but also would provide the sense of purpose he'd been missing at CyberBricks. It also sounded better than unemployment.

The prospect of joining the military had never crossed his mind before, but the idea grew on him. This could be his next big move—a fresh start in a role where he could genuinely serve his country.

He viewed the Navy's application form. "Fill out the application," Marvin said to his MetaMind. His AI assistant pulled in data from his resume and provided responses to some of the essay questions in the application. With a few clicks, his application was finished. He digitally submitted the form and smiled. He felt confident about his chances. After all, he was a staff engineer at CyberBricks, and much of the US government's cyber infrastructure used CyberBricks software.

4

Marvin dreamed of using his skills in a more dynamic, high-stakes environment. He waited for weeks, imagining the covert operations and cyber-espionage missions he'd undertake. And finally, he received an official correspondence from US Fleet Cyber Command:

> Thank you for your interest in the U.S. Navy's Cyber Specialty Direct Commission Program and especially for your desire to contribute to our Nation's defense. While your application was noteworthy, you have not been selected at this time as an officer candidate under this specialty program. However, you may possess skills that could be very beneficial to the cyberspace operations organizations defending the United States, and we encourage you to apply for civilian and military roles.

The rejection letter stung. His skills were top-notch, so why weren't they recognized? Marvin felt deflated.

"I thought it would be a great way to put my skills to use," Marvin thought. "Maybe I'm just not cut out for that kind of work."

5

Marvin Wong prided himself on his technical prowess, but when it came to the dating scene in San Francisco, the algorithms were not in his favor. Despite his wit, good manners, and his funny stories, he found himself sidelined in the city's dating Olympics. The gender imbalance was significant—according to the last census, there were 130 men to every 100 women in the 25-35 age group. To stand out, you needed to satisfy the "6666 rule": Have a six-figure salary, six-pack abs, be over six feet tall, and pack a 6-inch rocket. It wasn't easy being an average Joe in this high-stakes game.

Marvin, an Asian American with a modest height and a modest bank account, felt like a ghost in the dating world. Sure, he managed to snag a few dates, but they were as rare as a solar eclipse. And second dates? They might as well have been unicorns.

One evening, after paying for another date that would ultimately go nowhere, Marvin flopped onto his couch and put on his MetaMind. He swiped through dating profiles on his dating app. It was a numbers game, and he was losing.

But then, a lightbulb moment. What if he flipped the script? Instead of chasing after elusive matches, what the matches came to him?

In dating apps, he had to send digital roses and heart emojis to girls in hopes of getting a mutual match. But what if he engineered a funnel of interest coming to him, turning him into the chooser? He already understood basic marketing and sales conversion from his work with the sales team at CyberBricks. Maybe he could apply it to dating?

"I should start where most women spend their time in the metaverse," Marvin thought. "And approach this like a marketing funnel problem."

The most popular social media app was called InstaVR. Almost half of the planet logged in at least once per month to the app. Everyone had created an InstaVR account, whether you were Average Joe or a beautiful Hollywood actress. And with InstaVR, anyone could message anyone else who had a public profile page. Influencers on InstaVR messaged other influencers to make friends or get dates.

Marvin's InstaVR page was laughable, to put it mildly. He had about 300 followers composed of friends and family, and his photo and 3D videos featured scrapbook-like content from birthdays, trips, or restaurants. It looked like any average InstaVR account—nothing remarkable. And that's probably why girls he messaged on InstaVR weren't responding back.

Marvin downloaded an open source generative AI model to his MetaMind and provided it with a prompt: "Generate 30 high status images which feature me in them. Here are 100 photos of me for your training data. Final images should be appealing with an air of mystery.

Also refer to the top 100 most popular InstaVR profiles for inspiration."

The model studied Marvin's face from all angles and reconstructed him in various settings. The model outputted images of Marvin sitting at a fancy bar at a 5-star hotel sipping whiskey, getting out of an infinity pool in Singapore, sitting on the beach in Hawaii... The model even dressed him in expensive clothing and gave him facial hair. Marvin deleted the old content from his InstaVR page and uploaded these new photos, complete with AI-generated captions.

Marvin needed to increase his follower count. He funded his InstaVR advertising wallet with 300 FedCoins and started a generic advertising campaign to drive viewers to his page. The campaign began, and his follower count inched upwards by about 10 per minute.

In parallel, Marvin configured an automation AI model and connected it to his InstaVR account. He created a compound AI system by connecting the automation model to a convolutional neural network for image processing and a large language model for written tasks. He provided this prompt: "Here are 20 InstaVR accounts from women I find attractive. I want you to comb InstaVR and send a witty or clever opening message to them that references their last posted image."

Marvin ran a quick test to see how his bot operated. He watched as the bot sifted through profiles on InstaVR and sent messages. It had learned Marvin's tastes from the 20 training accounts he provided, and the crafted opening messages seemed genuine. Pleased with the results, Marvin instructed his MetaMind headset to continue running his AI script overnight with a goal to message 1000 InstaVR users by tomorrow morning. He had his outbound funnel.

Not stopping there, Marvin bought additional advertising credits on InstaVR. Instead of creating a generic ad campaign, he specified a target demographic. He specified age range, location, gender, and education level. For 500 FedCoins he could get his profile shown to 10,000 single women in San Francisco with a college degree or higher. He funded the marketing campaign, and InstaVR went to work. Marvin's photos began to show up in more users' homepages, and his follower count began to tick upwards. He had his inbound funnel.

Marvin took off his headset. "Well, that was fun. Let's see what happens tomorrow."

6

The following day, Marvin's MetaMind buzzed like a swarm of bees. Each message he received was a note in a symphony of new beginnings, but among the cacophony, one melody stood out: Grace Kim.

With a tap, Marvin found himself on Grace's InstaVR page, a digital diary of a life lived with elegance and zest. Her photos painted a portrait of a woman who danced between the worlds of academia and athleticism with the grace of a ballerina. Marvin was captivated. Her photos and videos portrayed a fascinating personality, and she was incredibly cute.

Her profile showcased a slender figure with a penchant for fitness, jet black hair cascading gracefully past her shoulders, and cute dimples when she smiled. They texted on InstaVR, and Marvin learned she was a 28 year-old medical student at University of California San Francisco. He was smitten.

Their conversation flowed effortlessly—shared interests in jazz, a mutual love for science fiction novels, and a keen interest in tech. Grace suggested they meet for a drink at a local jazz club.

That night, the atmosphere in the dimly lit jazz club was electric. The scent of aged wood and whiskey filled the air, the smooth tunes of the saxophone filling any gaps in conversation. When Grace walked in, Marvin felt his heart skip a beat. She looked even more beautiful in person.

"Marvin?" She approached with a slight tilt of her head, her defined eyebrows raised in inquiry.

"Hi Grace. Nice to meet you," Marvin replied, trying to sound more confident than he felt.

As they settled into a booth, Grace's interest in Marvin seemed genuine. She listened intently, laughed at his jokes, and shared her own fascinating tales. Her parents met at Seoul National University, but moved to California for work. She was a first-generation Korean American.

Marvin and Grace connected over their experiences growing up as Asian Americans in San Francisco. Grace attended Lowell High School, where she excelled. She had a particular flair for languages and world history, and spoke four languages. Grace was also very athletic, and standing at 5'8" she was taller than most women. Marvin couldn't help but notice how toned she was, and fought his urge to stare at her hourglass figure. She talked about her love for Judo and Muay Thai, finding them a unique blend of physical challenge and mental discipline.

While conversation was mostly lighthearted and fun, sometimes Grace's questions seemed oddly specific about Marvin's interests in cybersecurity—as if probing, searching for something deeper. Marvin brushed it off, attributing it to nerves.

Time flew by. They left the bar, and Marvin mustered up the courage to give Grace a goodnight kiss.

"I had fun," Grace said. "See you next time!"

Back in his apartment, Marvin grinned ear to ear. He was eager to see where this new connection with Grace would lead. She was incredible!

7

The budding relationship between Marvin and Grace had all the elements of an enchanting romance. Their dates ranged from hiking in the hills and watching the sunset over the Pacific to exploring hidden gem restaurants in the heart of San Francisco. With every moment they shared, Marvin felt himself more connected to her.

One evening, Marvin decided to bare his soul. They were at a rooftop bar by Union Square, the city's skyline twinkling below them. As the night deepened, Marvin's emotions poured out. He spoke of his dreams, his aspirations, and above all, his desire to make a difference.

"You know, Grace," he began hesitantly, taking a deep breath, "I've always felt this pull towards doing something bigger. My hacks… They're child's play really, and I only do them because they give me a thrill. I don't want to be just another hacker. I want to matter."

Grace listened intently. Encouraged by her silence, Marvin continued, "Sometimes I think I've chosen the wrong path. Like I was meant for something bigger… I'm paid well, but there's not much meaning in my work."

She reached across, taking his hand in hers. "Marvin, everyone has a calling. Maybe yours is just around the corner."

He looked into her eyes, getting lost in their depths. As the evening wore on, and the drinks flowed more freely, Marvin let his guard down. He spoke about his rejection from US Fleet Cyber Command and how that made him question his skills.

Grace, sensing an opening, leaned in closer. "Marvin," she whispered, her tone serious, "What if I told you there was a reason for everything? That our meeting wasn't just chance?"

He frowned, confused. "What do you mean?"

Grace took a deep breath, her demeanor changing. "Marvin, I'm not here by accident. I wasn't on InstaVR looking for love. I was looking for you."

She paused, gauging his reaction, "I work for the CIA. We've been watching you, Marvin. Your skills, your hacks. We see potential."

Marvin pulled back, disbelief clouding his eyes. "You used me? This was all a lie?"

Grace reached out, trying to hold his hand again, but he pulled away. "Not entirely," she murmured. "The mission was to get close to you, assess your loyalties. But Marvin, don't worry, I really did enjoy talking to you. You're a really nice guy."

He heard the words "nice guy" and felt like he'd been punched in his gut. It was a cocktail of disappointment, a drop in self esteem, and a bitter feeling of futility—all at once. "Dating in San Francisco sucks," he said, looking away, but unable to hide his frustration.

Grace continued, her voice soft yet firm, "The country needs you, Marvin. You talk about wanting to serve, wanting to matter. This is your chance."

He shook his head, feeling betrayed. "And what if I refuse? What if I just want to go back to my normal life?"

Grace's face hardened. "America is facing a cyber threat unlike anything we've seen before. You asked for an opportunity, you got it. You have 48 hours to decide. If you're in, call me. If not, don't bother."

Marvin stared at her, a whirlwind of emotions coursing through him. Anger, betrayal, sadness, but also a flicker of excitement. Maybe this was the calling he had been waiting for?

8

Marvin sat in the corner of his room, the glow from his desk lamp casting long shadows across the walls filled with bookshelves and gadgets. The room was a testament to a life spent pursuing knowledge and skill, a sanctuary for a mind always searching for more. His parents, who were frequently absent due to their demanding jobs, had unintentionally gifted him the freedom to explore his interests. He had become a navigator of the shadowy corners of the internet, a wizard in the realms of code and cybersecurity. As a child, he learned how to browse the dark web and download video games illegally.

At school, Marvin had learned to game the system. Achieving top grades had become a tactical choice rather than a pursuit of excellence. He noticed that teachers favored the top performing students. These students were left to their own devices and labeled as "gifted and talented." So Marvin worked just enough to get into the top 10% of his class. Here, he realized, he could exist without drawing unwanted attention or pressure. He earned straight-As, but cared little about what he was actually learning.

His parents' hands-off approach to parenting was in stark contrast to the stereotypical "Tiger parenting" his Asian friends experienced. Marvin's parents had allowed him the space to grow independently, to cultivate skills beyond the traditional curriculum, but it had also left him without a guiding hand, without someone to share in the triumphs and trials of his unique journey. Perhaps his parents were too busy with work to worry about his upbringing, but he was largely left to his own devices.

Now, as Marvin sat pondering the chance to join the CIA, he realized that his entire life had been a preparation for this moment. The prospect of joining the intelligence community wasn't just a career change; it was a leap into a world that most people only saw in movies. He had grown up watching those very films, enthralled by the world of espionage, double agents, and adrenaline-filled missions.

The conventional path lay before him, comfortable and predictable. He could just keep doing what he was doing for the next 20 years—coding and vesting private sector stock, earning private sector pay and maybe one day get his name on a few patents at work. He'd be materially comfortable, and perhaps encounter a few stimulating challenges at work that pushed his skills. But his life would unfold, more or less, like many of the people he knew 20 years ahead of him. A nice house, nice car, family, and two vacations per year. Nothing wrong with that life, but was it the life he wanted?

The other path was murky and fraught with danger. It was a road less traveled, filled with unknown challenges —and potential death. Marvin couldn't help but feel a surge of adrenaline at the thought. The unknown was where he thrived, where his skills could be truly tested.

He picked up his phone and dialed Grace "Hey, I'm in. How do we make this happen?"

Grace's voice was calm and measured. "Wonderful. I'm going to call Headquarters to arrange everything. You're not actually going to leave your job. They'll put you on paid administrative leave and the government will pay your employer to keep you on payroll, plus a little extra to make it worth their while. On paper, you'll still work for your cybersecurity company, but you'll be one of us now. You'll receive an encrypted phone and a laptop. Look out for that in the next few days."

Marvin tried to match her calmness. "Thanks, Grace. Oh, one last thing."

"What is it?" replied Grace.

"My manager at CyberBricks a real ass. He's trying to get me fired right now, so he might protest if we force this plan on him."

"Oh don't worry about that stuff. We know about your PIP. You're being promoted to principal engineer in the Department of Special Projects which gets most of its funding from government contracts. Your manager won't be a problem anymore. We've got your back."

Grace hung up. Marvin poured himself a glass of whiskey and pondered his decision. The moment felt like both an end and a beginning. He was leaving behind a life of predictability for a chance to truly make a difference, to use his skills in ways he never imagined. Thus closed the chapter on Marvin's old life, and a new, thrilling adventure began.

9

Fort Meade, Maryland
Day 1 of CIA Cyber Officer Training

The early morning reveille tore through the still dawn, pulling recruits from their dreams. Marvin, bleary-eyed and groggy, stumbled out of his bunk and joined the ranks. The first weeks were the hardest. Every day began with an hourlong swim, push-ups, sit-ups, pull-ups, and a 3-mile run. His muscles ached in places he didn't know existed. But with each passing day, he felt stronger, his endurance grew, and his body transformed.

Marvin knew training wouldn't be easy, but nothing could have prepared him for this. His training was a collaboration between the CIA and the Navy, beginning with an accelerated program at the United States Fleet Cyber Command in Fort Meade.

Marvin had to learn hand-to-hand combat. He was introduced to a blend of martial arts including Brazilian Jiu-Jitsu, Krav Maga, and Karate. Brazilian Jiu-Jitsu taught him ground fighting and the importance of leverage. Krav Maga focused on neutralizing threats swiftly and efficiently. And Karate honed his striking skills. Marvin learned to disarm opponents, break holds, and apply devastating counters.

Handgun training was next. The kickback of the gun initially startled Marvin, but with expert guidance, he mastered aiming and shooting with precision. Day after day, Marvin felt a transformation, not just in his skills but also in his mindset.

While mornings were dedicated to the physical aspect of his training, afternoons were focused on cyber training. Here, Marvin felt more at home. But the stakes were much higher. The Navy's vast cyber infrastructure was a complex web of networks, systems, and protocols. He was introduced to state-of-the-art cyber tools and resources. Every exercise was a race against time: cracking codes, reinforcing firewalls, and simulating cyber-attacks to test the infrastructure's resilience.

Marvin was paired with Lieutenant Rickard, a seasoned Navy cyber officer. Rickard became his mentor, pushing him to his limits. They spent hours on coding drills, where Marvin had to hack into dummy systems or find vulnerabilities in supposedly secure networks.

One memorable task had Marvin trying to break into a mock naval server. Hours turned into days, but Marvin was relentless. Instead of using a traditional keyboard to type out his hacks, the Navy gave him a special NeuraVisor headset that could understand his intent and write code at the speed of thought. It took some getting used to, but it was oddly satisfying for Marvin to think of code and suddenly see it written in front of him. NeuraVisor also included an advanced AI assistant that understood how to debug and write code, so Marvin made good use of it by delegating simple coding tasks to it while he worked on harder problems. The visor, like the MetaMind, allowed Marvin to code across dozens of virtual computer screens. But NeuraVisor used advanced thought-tracking to immediately infer which code block he wanted to work on—it could understand his brain signals. He was able to code at the speed of thought, and with the AI assistant, he could easily perform the work of 10 software engineers.

But even with the NeuraVisor and all its AI support, the work was grueling. He put in 18-hour days—just enough time to wolf down a few bites of food in between hacks, go to the bathroom, and sleep for a few hours. By the end of three days of this routine, his mind and body felt numb. He could barely keep his eyes open, but he had to keep pushing. His mind was so tired and his thoughts so scattered that the NeuraVisor stopped working. By the end of the third day, he abandoned the visor and just wrote code like it was 2030—with an old-fashioned mouse, keyboard, and a computer screen. It felt like his fingers typed out code purely on instinct. His mind was on its last legs, but he had to break into the system...

He wrote his last line of code and hit ENTER. A progress bar sped across the screen, and suddenly a secure shell opened up with access to the server's backend systems. He was in.

Rickard, impressed, patted him on the back, "You passed, kid!"

Weekends brought no respite. They were reserved for mock field missions, simulating real-world scenarios where cyber officers worked in tandem with soldiers in the field. These missions were designed to be unpredictable. In one mission, Marvin had to deploy with a SEAL team in enemy territory in the woods southwest of Fort Meade. Using a ruggedized laptop, radio, and satellite data connection, he ran hacks to confuse enemy detection systems or misdirect search teams.

Despite the grueling regimen, there were moments of camaraderie and fun. The bond between recruits grew strong, a brotherhood forged in the fires of discipline and determination. They shared stories around campfires, pushed each other during drills, and looked out for each other during training.

10

"Today, we learn singleton CQB," said the drill instructor. "Pick up your rifle and get ready."

CQB stood for "close-quarters battle." Whenever entering a hostile building or navigating tight spaces outdoors, teams would use specialized team CQB tactics to safely navigate unknown areas and clear them of threats. Teamwork was essential in CQB because one person could only check so much space for threats upon entry before alerting the enemy in that room. If you entered the room and checked right, but the enemy was in a corner on the left, you died. You relied on the man next to you to check the other corner, and if he didn't—you both died. Singleton CQB was a variant of CQB where you had to clear hostile space entirely on your own.

"Sir, why singleton CQB?" asked Marvin. "I'm a cyber specialist, I'm never going to be clearing buildings on my own. I doubt I'd even be behind enemy lines—my role is in front of a computer, not behind a rifle."

"You're lucky you're such a good hacker, or I'd have you run five miles just for asking that stupid question," said the instructor. "But I'll entertain your question today only. My job is to prepare you for worst-case scenarios. Sure, you may never get deployed into a hostile building. You may never need to go room to room to clear space and shoot at enemies. But let me ask you something—what happens if you're driving to your mission objective in a hostile area, and an explosive blows up your vehicle and you're the only one left? What if you're separated from your squad? You need to be ready to shoot your way through hostile parts of the city to get to the safe zone, which could be miles away. Let's say you're busy coding behind that NeuraVisor, and an enemy SpecOps soldier infiltrates your safe house and kills your team in the other room. In those situations, it's kill or be killed. You have to either secure the building yourself or shoot your way out to safety. You cannot rely on your team to always be there."

Marvin nodded. It made sense—he had to be ready for anything in the field. He picked up an E-Coil rifle, chambered in 7.62mm. The gun auto-chambered a dummy round, and a red LED on the back indicated it was a loaded weapon.

The E-Coil was a technical marvel. Unlike the bullets of the early 21st century, E-Coil rounds didn't use gunpowder. These were caseless rounds that left behind no residue or brass casings when fired. The E-Coil featured a barrel wrapped with a metal coil. When the shooter pulled the trigger, the gun delivered a massive jolt of electricity to the coil. The coils used a magnetic field to deliver 465 joules of kinetic energy to a 10-gram round, resulting in an exiting muzzle velocity of 1,000 feet per second. The muzzle velocity could be dialed up or down by the user based on need—higher speeds for supersonic armor-piercing capability, and slower speeds if you wanted to prevent wall over-penetration in dense urban areas. But 1,000 feet per second provided whisper-quiet subsonic rounds that could still beat armor. It was the perfect speed for stealth and lethality.

During training and CQB drills, the gun was loaded with a special dummy round and the gun's magnetic coil was turned off. A small hammer in the dummy round would knock back and forth with each trigger pull, simulating the recoil of a discharged bullet. An infrared laser at the front of the gun would mark hits, and all soldiers wore a special infrared-sensitive suit that would apply a painful jolt of electricity wherever they were hit. It was like a laser tag game, except the pain was real.

Marvin had to practice dozens of different door approach and entry scenarios. While clearing rooms, closed doors required special care. First, the breacher had no idea what was on the other side of the door. One could listen carefully for sounds or scout through windows to get hints, but in a real-world scenario you rarely had that luxury. Additionally, once stealth was compromised, one often needed to make split-second judgements and go room to room without hesitation.

He learned that standard entry doors had a strong side and weak side. For a door that opened away from the breacher, the "strong side" was nearest the door hinges (some refer to this as "hinge side" to avoid ambiguity), while the "weak side" was on the side nearest to the doorknob (also called the "knob side"). They were named "strong" and "weak" to indicate which side is better to be standing with a readied weapon if the door was opened. The strong side offered the easiest view into the room, while the weak side view was obstructed by the door as it was opened.

It was counterintuitive, but Marvin learned that it was advantageous to stand on the weak side of the door if performing singleton CQB with a door that opened away from you. This allowed you to open the door and push it outwards. While the door swung out, you had some time to back up and ready your rifle from concealment. If you tried to open the door on the strong side during solo CQB, you might reveal yourself to the room before you have time to aim your rifle.

Wide open doors were easier to work with, since you no longer needed to worry about opening the door and readying your weapon in a short time. You could approach an open door with a readied weapon and choose your angle of attack.

He practiced a technique called "slicing the pie," also known as PIE technique. The concept was simple—Marvin used one edge of the doorframe as the center of a pie, and imagined pie slices extending out into the room. As he approached the door, he started near the wall and checked the narrow slices along the far inner wall. As he gradually moved closer to the door threshold, he checked some of the angles that peered farther into the distant half of the room. He was careful not to extend his rifle barrel through the door threshold which would reveal himself to enemies in the room. He quickly checked the middle of the room and then swept the back half of the room. After clearing as much as he could from outside the door, he stepped inside and quickly checked corners for any missed enemies.

The PIE technique was easy to perform in ideal situations. If doors were closed or stealth was compromised, the breacher would need to adjust the slicing process or make snap judgements about where to compromise thoroughness in order to clear a room quickly. Textbook technique was great in the classroom, but once bullets started flying a soldier had to trust his instincts and move. Because doors and entryways could be on any side of a room, obstacles often got in the way of ideal door clearing technique. A breacher couldn't open a door from the knob side if a refrigerator was positioned there, for instance. Sometimes Marvin had to improvise and clear a room with suboptimal conditions.

The training was painful. Every time Marvin stuck his weapon out too far into a doorway or forgot to check a corner, he was punished with an onslaught of simulated gunfire. But eventually he internalized the training, and room clearing felt natural. His muscle memory kicked in when he encountered unusual door arrangements. After a week of drills, the drill instructor gave him a passing score.

"Marvin," said the drill instructor. "Singleton CQB is not ideal and there's a very good chance you'll get shot even if you do it all perfectly. But you've learned well, and it's about time for you to deploy. Good luck."

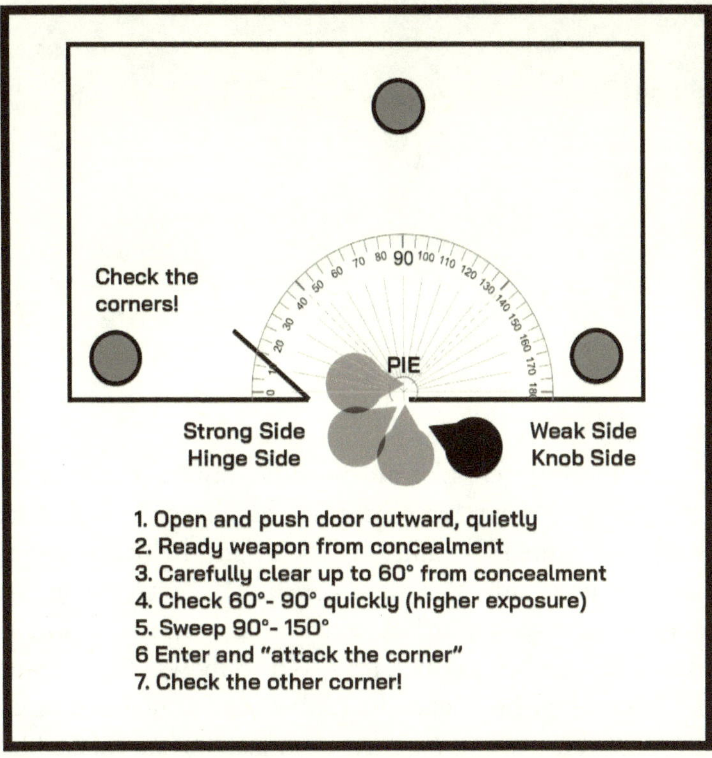

Notes from Marvin's Singleton CQB training.

11

Three months felt like an eternity, but as the training concluded, Marvin felt proud. He had been pushed to his limits both mentally and physically, and he had emerged on the other side as a new person. The once sedentary coder was now a warrior, ready to defend his nation in the digital and physical realms. Not only was he far more fit than when he began (he added six pounds of muscle through the training regimen), but also he had pushed his hacking and coding skills further than ever before.

Despite his achievements, Marvin's graduation from the program was a silent affair. There was no ceremony. His transformation was a clandestine operation, conducted away from the public eye and absent from any official records. The CIA had sought to create a weapon honed in secrecy, and in Marvin they had succeeded.

The absence of formal recognition did not diminish Marvin's sense of accomplishment. If anything, it reinforced the covert nature of his new role and the critical importance of his upcoming missions.

Heading to Langley, Marvin was acutely aware of the weight of his responsibilities. He was no longer just a programmer; he was a cyber operative trained to face the multifaceted threats of the modern world. His path forward was clear, albeit shrouded in the secrecy that his profession demanded. As he left the military base, Marvin felt a mix of anticipation and resolve. The challenges ahead were many, but he was ready to meet them head-on with the skills and knowledge he had acquired. He was ready to defend his nation in cyberspace and on the battlefield.

12

Langley, Virginia

Grace leaned against the door frame, a smirk playing on her lips. "Congrats, Marvin," she began, "on becoming a bona fide CIA Cyber Officer. Not everyone makes the cut."

Marvin looked up from his laptop, suddenly feeling underdressed. Grace was the epitome of sophistication in a sleek black turtleneck and dark leather pants, looking like she had stepped straight out of a fashion magazine. In contrast, Marvin, who had just arrived from bootcamp the night before, had bought a blue collared shirt and brown slacks from a discount department store that morning.

"Thanks, Grace," he said, "though I admit I'm no field operative like you."

Grace laughed, "That's true! But that's why you're behind the screen and I'm in the field."

Before Marvin could respond, Grace beckoned him. "Let's go. We've got a meeting with Director Lin."

It was a 10 minute walk to Director Lin's office at the other side of campus. Marvin felt nervous.

"What should I know about Lin?" he asked Grace as they descended a stairwell.

"He's a bit of a jaded old man, kind of like every CIA director you see in a Hollywood movie," said Grace. "But he's trustworthy. Really worked his way up the ranks over the decades. He actually grew up not far from where you're from."

"Oh really? What's his background?"

"He's Taiwanese American, originally from Rowland Heights in California. His family immigrated to the US around the 1980s. He's been with the CIA most of his career. He spent two decades in the field, and the last 10 years in leadership positions in Langley. He's been a longtime friend of President Phelps, they went to college together. The reason Phelps didn't nominate him as VP is because the polls showed America wasn't ready to have an East Asian that close to the Presidency."

"Not much has changed," Marvin said, remembering what his parents told him about the bamboo ceiling.[1]

"Yep, but nobody minds when we run things behind the scenes," Grace winked. "Oh and whatever you do, don't bullshit Director Lin. Just tell him things as they are, without sugar coating."

Marvin and Grace made their way through the narrow, polished corridors, finally arriving at a large mahogany door marked "CIA Director." Marvin took a deep breath, trying to calm his racing heart.

---

[1] The "bamboo ceiling" is a term popularized by Jane Hyun in 2005 which refers to the barriers many Asian Americans seemed to face when aspiring to leadership positions in Western organizations.

The office was spacious and imposing. Director Lin sat behind a vast, immaculate desk, his intense eyes assessing Marvin.

Director Lin was a tall, slender man in his late fifties, with a dignified air that commanded respect. His hair, a mix of salt and pepper, was neatly combed back, revealing a high forehead and a few deep lines etched by years of service and experience. He wore a tailored charcoal gray suit that accentuated his lean frame, paired with a crisp white shirt and a navy blue tie. Despite his formal attire, there was a subtle hint of approachability in his demeanor. A discreet American flag pin on his lapel and a polished wristwatch completed his distinguished look, making it clear that Director Lin was not just a bureaucrat, but a sophisticated professional.

"This is the guy?" Lin's voice was gravelly, full of authority. "The one you've been telling me about?"

Grace nodded, a tinge of pride in her voice. "Yes, sir. Finished his boot camp and passed the Cyber Officer Exam. Best score in a decade."

Lin raised an eyebrow. "Best kiss in a decade too?"

A flush crept over Grace's face, but she kept her composure. "Sir, we should maintain a level of professionalism here. It was a necessary step to ensure his allegiance. And, for the record, he's decent."

Marvin shifted uncomfortably. This was not how he thought his first meeting with the Director would start.

Lin, sensing the tension, chuckled. "Alright, let's get down to business. We have intel that suggests China has embarked on a secret project. We've managed to locate an informant in the dark web who claims to have the details we need."

"You want me to make contact?" asked Marvin.

Grace interjected, "Yes, but not in the way you might think. You won't be using the usual channels. This informant has a unique method of communication. You'll need to log in to an encrypted videogame session using a MetaMind headset."

Marvin gulped. "Alright. What's the informant's alias?"

"Golden Rat," Grace replied. "And you'll be Titanium Dragon. He's expecting you. Remember to anonymize your voice when you talk to him."

Marvin was determined. He may not have Grace's field experience, but he was a whiz behind the screen. With the weight of this mission on his shoulders, he'd prove to everyone, especially himself, that he deserved the title of CIA Cyber Officer.

As they left Director Lin's office, the gravity of the situation began to sink in. The coming week would be a whirlwind of activity. Marvin was ready for the challenge.

13

Lat: 21.451115, Long: 111.314543

The cold sting of the South China Sea nipped at Grace's cheeks as she cruised underwater towards her destination. Her heart pounded, not out of fear but from the adrenaline pumping through her veins. She had to follow a 1.5 mile rock wall that outlined the artificial bay. Once near shore, she'd reach the coordinates and search for clues.

Her underwater jetpack system made her as agile as a dolphin, darting through the water with ease. She donned an oxygen rebreather and combat swimmer wetsuit, and carried a silenced 9mm handgun on her hip.

As she approached the end of the rock wall, Grace slowed her propulsion system. The stillness of the night was occasionally disrupted by the muted sounds of distant vehicles. She chose a secluded spot to climb ashore, and stashed her fins and gear behind some large rocks.

By design, she approached on a dark, moonless night. Her night vision goggles revealed an entrance to a deep cave. She began her cautious advance.The cave was massive—at least one football field wide, and the water just as deep. None of this was visible from the outside—it was perfectly hidden under the artificial rock wall of the bay.

Suddenly, a deep rumbling echoed from the cave, shaking the water around her. Grace quickly found cover behind a rock outcropping, her eyes darting to the source of the sound.

Emerging from the cave was a massive, dark structure. It looked like a submarine, but not one she had seen or heard of before. As it glided smoothly past her, she noted the sleek, futuristic design.

Not wasting a moment, Grace activated a compact scanning device on her wrist. The device hummed softly, capturing electromagnetic and thermal data from the strange submarine. She toggled the recording mode on her goggles, ensuring she had visual evidence to go along with the scans.

But the cave's opening did not only reveal the submarine. Soldiers regularly patrolled catwalks and doorways inside. The ordinary looking rock wall hid a research and development lab. The real base, an underground facility that extended deep inland, likely held hundreds of researchers and soldiers.

Grace knew that infiltration was no longer an option. There were too many soldiers. She gathered as much intel as she could from the cave and headed back to equip her swim gear.

Reactivating her underwater propulsion system, Grace retreated into the ocean, evading detection. As the currents carried her away, an unsettling feeling lingered within her.

As she made her way back to her extraction point, one thought was clear in her mind: Marvin and the rest of her team needed to see what she had found.

A mysterious submarine departs a secret Chinese dock.

Part Two

Quantum Prelude

1

Hubei, China (2010)

Amidst the lush, undulating landscape of rural Hubei, Zheng Song Han spent his days tending to the family farm. Their rice fields stretched as far as the eye could see. But young Zheng, just 10 years old, felt there might be more to life than the bucolic land he saw before him.

Zheng's parents were a study in contrasts to the gentle curves of the countryside, embodying the harsh realities that often come with rural living. His father, a towering figure of unwavering principles, believed in the tough love approach to parenting. He saw potential in Zheng but was often quick to call him a disappointment, his words slicing through Zheng's spirit like a scythe. Slaps and belt whippings were common—Zheng's father disciplined him just as his father had before him. But it was all done out of love, Zheng told himself. His father just wanted to steer him to greatness. "You must be stronger, smarter, better," his father would say, his voice echoing against the walls of their modest home, "You are meant for more than this farm."

Zheng's mother may have loved him, but she did not show it. She believed in the tangible results of hard work and often resorted to hitting Zheng with a stick when her words failed to leave an impression. It was a tough love born out of fear; fear that without strict guidance, Zheng would falter in a world that was much less forgiving than the countryside.

Zheng's parents wanted more for their son than a life bound to the soil. They saw the farm as a beginning, not an end—a foundation of hard work and resilience on which Zheng could build a future far beyond the rural confines of his upbringing. Their strictness was fueled by a desperate hope for their son to transcend the limitations they themselves could not escape.

Life in rural China had become bleak. The Shanghai Composite Index had fallen over 30% since October 2007, and the country's exports had declined dramatically. Consumers in Europe and the United States cut back on spending, and China paid the price. The Global Financial Crisis may have started in the West, but its effects could be felt even by a hungry child in rural China.

The schoolhouse Zheng attended was a simple brick structure, its walls adorned with images of heroic figures from China's past. It was within these walls that Zheng's world view started to take shape.

Each lesson taught him something new about his nation's history. Zheng, with a thirst for knowledge, lapped up every word, every narrative, every detail of China's past glories and defeats.

One afternoon, as the sun cast long shadows on the playground, Zheng's teacher began the lesson on China's "century of national humiliation"—a period that began with the First Opium War in 1839 and ended with the establishment of the People's Republic of China in 1949. The First Opium War, largely fought to stop the British from importing thousands of pounds of opium into China, resulted in the British occupation of Hong Kong in 1841. To add insult to injury, the British pressured the Qing Empire to sign the Treaty of Nanking which ceded Hong Kong to Britain. Zheng was also surprised to learn that Germany had seized Tsingtao in 1897, only to surrender the city to the Japanese at the end of WWI. Everybody wanted a piece of China, and the impotent Qing Empire was powerless to stop foreigners from carving up the country.

Did every country use China as its playground? Hong Kong, Tsingtao, Manchuria... were all lost to foreigners. Zheng learned that China had been humbled, time and again, by powers that sought to exploit its vastness, its resources, its people.

He grew more resolute with each passing year. These memories, these tales of oppression, fueled his ambition. Zheng believed that for China to rise, it could not rely on the goodwill of outsiders. It had to be strong, unified, and impenetrable. Most importantly, China had to free itself from foreign exploitation.

Everyday after school, Zheng watched his classmates leave class to greet their parents near the schoolhouse gate. Zheng's parents were never there, and the first thing he'd hear when he got home was, "Finish your chores!" His parents never attended his graduation ceremonies.

As he grew older, the farm could no longer contain his aspirations. He sought higher education and made his way to the prestigious Tsinghua University, where he double majored in economics and computer science.[2] His professors, noticing his ability apply artificial intelligence and algorithmic thinking to problems in economics, encouraged him to consider a career in public policy.

But Zheng wanted a different path. He believed that China needed a strong military to protect its economy and borders from foreign interference. Zheng became obsessed with the idea of enhancing military capabilities with artificial intelligence. He participated in a PLA Navy co-op program, studying military tactics and history while simultaneously completing his undergraduate studies. He completed his civilian education and transferred to Dalian Naval Academy for full-time officer training.

At Dalian, Zheng's strategic acumen and leadership qualities quickly set him apart. Zheng excelled in military strategy, and he quickly rose to prominence thanks to his discipline and intellectual acuity. Zheng graduated from Dalian with high honors and served in different ship rotations in the East Sea Fleet.

By 2045, Zheng had reached the position of Vice Admiral, a role in which he demonstrated not only military prowess but also a keen understanding of geopolitical dynamics. His strategies in naval engagements and his contributions to maritime security significantly enhanced China's territorial sovereignty and global maritime influence. He commanded the East Sea Fleet from 2045 - 2050 and helped China navigate

[2] Tsinghua University (清華大學) in Beijing is often regarded as the MIT of China. Notable alumni include Xi Jinping (chemical engineering, Class of 1979) and Hu Jintao (hydraulic engineering, Class of 1964). Less than 1% of applicants are accepted each year.

through numerous high profile conflicts near Taiwan, Japan, and the Philippines.

2

Beijing (2020)

Chen Yi grew up in the heart of Beijing, under the sprawling shadows of ancient temples juxtaposed with the gleaming facades of modern skyscrapers. His dreams stretched as far as the city's skyline. From a young age, he dreamed of exploring the world beyond the walls of his claustrophobic city.

Yi's high school years were characterized by a youthful optimism and a blossoming romance with Cheng Xiao, a girl whose laughter could light up the drab corridors of their school. Their love story was the talk of their classmates—Xiao, with her quick wit and radiant smile, complemented Yi's serious and studious nature perfectly. Together, they dreamt of a future bright with promise, walking hand in hand through the Beijing night markets.

Upon graduating high school, Yi, fueled by a desire to serve his country and carve out a name for himself, decided to join officer candidate school at Dalian Naval Academy. It was a decision made with a heavy heart, knowing the distance it would place between him and

Xiao. Yet, with tearful goodbyes and promises of unwavering loyalty, they vowed to overcome the challenges of separation. Xiao's parting words, "I'll wait for you," kept Yi going in the demanding days that followed.

The military academy was a world apart from anything Yi had known. The rigorous training, strict discipline, and unrelenting demands tested every fiber of his being. Yet, he thrived, driven by the vision of the life he yearned to build with Xiao. Letters from her were his lifeline, a reminder of the world beyond the academy's imposing walls.

However, two years into his training, the letters began to dwindle, and the calls became strained. As a novel coronavirus swept through China in 2020, it became impossible to visit Xiao. They tried phone calls, but Xiao's voice, once warm and familiar, seemed distant. And then one day, the calls stopped. Voicemails were unanswered. He never heard from her again.

His friends told him she was dating a wealthy businessman, someone who could offer her the world Yi had only dreamt of giving her. The breakup was a crucible, burning away the remnants of Yi's youthful naivety and leaving in its wake a steely determination. Pain was his teacher. At the academy gym, he pushed himself to lift one extra set, or do one extra push-up, or swim one extra lap—the physical pain distracting him from his heartache and disappointment. With every drop of sweat and every muscle strained, he vowed to rise above his circumstances, to become a man of strength and honor. To become the man Xiao would regret leaving.

His efforts did not go unnoticed. Yi excelled academically and physically, dominating his class and earning the respect of both peers and superiors. His singular focus and unparalleled dedication caught the eye of his commanders, paving the way for his early assignment to *Changzheng 20*, an ultra modern nuclear submarine, as a Communications Officer—a coveted first assignment.[3] He dreamed of being the captain of his own submarine one day, and he knew that this first assignment would help gain him the experience and connections needed to rise up in the ranks.

Stepping aboard the *Changzheng 20* was a moment of profound significance for Yi. The submarine, a marvel of military engineering, represented the culmination of his years of sacrifice and hard work. As the hatch closed behind him, sealing him in the steel behemoth that would be his home for the foreseeable future, Yi felt a chapter of his life closing with it. It was 2022, and China was also exiting the pandemic. Although China struggled with the economic challenges of recovery, Yi's livelihood was secure in the military. While most of his friends in Beijing found themselves unemployed and listless in the difficult years after the pandemic, Yi's career flourished aboard *Changzheng 20*.

The submarine's confined quarters and the constant hum of machinery became the backdrop to Yi's new life. In the bowels of the ocean, where daylight was a memory and silence a luxury, Yi found a sense of peace. Nothing else mattered when you were onboard the submarine—all the problems on the mainland gave way to the ocean

---

[3] In the PLA Navy, submarines are simply named *Changzheng* (长征), followed by the ship number. *Changzheng* means "long march" in English.

abyss. His role as Communications Officer was critical, the lifeline between the submarine and the world above. It demanded precision, calm under pressure, and an unwavering focus.

Yet, as the submarine glided through the dark waters, a part of Yi's heart still felt the past. Xiao's memory, though faded, was etched into his being, a bittersweet reminder of what had been and what could never be again. But it was this very heartbreak that had sculpted him into the man he had become—a man of resilience, of unwavering resolve, and of a desire to serve a higher calling.

As Yi sat at his post, eyes fixed on the instruments before him, he realized that the journey ahead was fraught with challenges and uncertainties. Yet, he felt ready. The heartbreak that had once threatened to consume him had instead ignited a flame within, propelling him forward into the depths and darkness, towards a destiny that was only just beginning to unfold. In the silent world beneath the waves, Yi had found his purpose, forged by the fires of loss and tempered by the resolve never to falter again.

3

Taiwan Today, Asia Tomorrow

By Grace Kim
East Asian Studies, Spring 2047 - UC Berkeley

For decades, people around the world have asked the question, "Is this the year China invades Taiwan?" It's an event which everyone hopes to avoid, yet simultaneously acts as if it is inevitable.

China has tried numerous times to subvert the democratic process in Taiwan to find a diplomatic path to reunification. It has provided shadow funding to Taiwan's Reunification Party since 2035. And yet, despite all attempts to influence elections through campaign spending and bribes, it has not yet been able to achieve more than a small caucus of 11 seats in the Legislative Yuan. A recent crackdown on corruption has landed several Reunification Party members in jail. And while the Reunification Party, and its shadow leadership in the Chinese Communist Party (CCP), have influenced some votes to lean towards reunification, progress has stalled. The Taiwanese people truly wish to be free of China's grip, and the CCP now contemplates more direct paths to reunification.

Cross-strait relations are at their lowest in twenty years, largely caused by China's military buildup around the East China Sea and the Taiwan Strait. The East Sea Fleet in the People's Liberation Army Navy (PLAN) underwent major modernization in the last 25 years with the addition of two nuclear submarines and two fully-loaded aircraft carriers. According to publicly available estimates from the US Congressional Research Service, the 2047 East Sea Fleet is composed of these ships (weapons classification in parentheses):

```
16 Destroyers (nuclear capable)
20 Frigates (conventional)
5 Nuclear-powered attack submarines (conventional)
2 Nuclear-powered attack submarines (nuclear armed)
10 Diesel-electric attack submarines (conventional)
2 Aircraft carriers (each carries 70-100 aircraft)
20 Amphibious ships (transport)
6 Replenishment ships
2 Hospital ships
2 Submarine support ships
```

Additionally, the PLA Air Force has gradually increased its surface-launched ballistic missile capabilities. From 300 conventional medium-range ballistic missiles (MRBMs) in 2024, China has gradually increased its armament to about 800 MRBMs today. Approximately 500 of China's MRBMs are within striking distance of Taiwan. China's conventional MRBMs have a blast radius of 1-1.5 kilometers and have sufficient impact velocity to bust through bunkers and fortifications. With the push of a button, China could fire 50 MRBMs at each of Taiwan's military airfields with plenty to spare. Taiwan's aging Patriot II system would intercept 30-50% of these

MRBMs, but at least half would break through and hit their targets.

Nevertheless, I am ruling out a direct military engagement between Taiwan and China. First, China does not wish to absorb a destroyed country. A widespread MRBM bombardment and a ground-based invasion would turn Taiwan into a liability rather than an asset. Cities would burn, people would starve, and the humanitarian crisis would earn the condemnation of the international community. China observed Russia's difficulties staging a land invasion in Ukraine and wishes to avoid being pulled into a similar conflict.

Second, military conflict would only occur if either Taiwan or the West attacked first. Taiwan's military has access to the same data that we have about China's military. It knows that it is outgunned. It also knows that China could launch 500 MRBMs in less than 15 minutes—faster than any Western power could intervene. The East Sea Fleet could unleash a barrage of stealth long-range anti-ship missiles which would sink the majority of Taiwan's aging navy in one strike.

Taiwan invested heavily in defensive assets in the 2010s when the Chinese military had not yet achieved parity with modern navies. Taiwan's fast-attack missile boats were formidable against the PLA Navy of the 2010s and 2020s, but Chinese military innovation has since leapfrogged even that of the West's best militaries. Additionally, the United States has proven itself an unreliable partner in overseas conflicts over the last few decades. Alternating between attitudes of isolationism and globalism, the US's appetite to defend small democracies like Taiwan ebbs and flows with the political cycle. The argument that the US will save Taiwan to preserve access to semiconductors and AI chips is weak—the US has had several decades to diversify its semiconductor supply chain away from Taiwan, and likely would not risk an all-out war with China for semiconductors.

Taiwan invested in the Hai Kun class fast attack submarine in 2020, with the first of 8 commissioned in 2025. These diesel-electric attack submarines are no match for China's newest nuclear-powered attack submarines. The Hai Kun's stealth posed a moderate threat to China's rudimentary nuclear submarines of the 2020s (which were about as loud as USSR submarines in the 1970s), but the advantage has faded over the decades. China's East Sea Fleet currently sports 10 diesel-electric attack submarines, as well as 7 ultra-quiet nuclear submarines. War game simulations performed by the US Navy suggest that China could eliminate Taiwan's entire submarine fleet with just three of its nuclear submarines.

Taiwan could survive an initial attack if it had the support of the West. By 2030, however, it became clear that most Western countries had lost their appetite for war. The United States significantly reduced its involvement in overseas conflict throughout the 2020s. After its hasty withdrawal from Afghanistan, the United States adopted a strategy of equipping proxy countries with deterrence weapons rather than sending troops. It outfitted Taiwan with Patriot missiles, Harpoons, Sidewinders, Stingers, HIMARs, torpedoes, and drones. These weapons offer fantastic self-defensive capabilities, but offer little deep-strike capability. They are porcupine weapons—they hurt you if you invade, but are harmless to you from afar. The United States finally allowed Taiwan to purchase F-35s in the 2030s, which provided

Taiwan with deep strike capability. But by then, China had developed very strong anti-air and anti-stealth technology, and the F-35's advantages were severely diminished.

Taiwan depended on the F-35 for air superiority, but in 2047 the aircraft is showing its age. China's Chengdu J-22, a sixth-generation fighter jet, has surpassed the F-35's stealth and electronic warfare capabilities. Taiwan's Air Force might stand a chance against China if supported by Patriot II surface-to-air missiles sites. However, it is expected that China's initial attack would destroy the majority of Patriot II sites and landing strips, and cripple the Taiwanese navy. Without backup, Taiwan's F-35 fleet would eventually die from attrition. Meanwhile, China could easily resupply J-22s from its two aircraft carriers nearby or from mainland bases.

Since it is unlikely the West would step in to defend Taiwan, we must assume that Taiwan is on its own to defend against any Chinese incursion. If we rule out a land invasion (which would pull China into a Ukraine-like boondoggle), and rule out a voluntary political reunification process, there is one viable and likely path China could take: a blockade.

China has two options to enact a blockade: 1) It could deploy the East Sea Fleet to enforce a military blockade just outside of Taiwan's territorial waters or 2) Deploy an informal blockade under the guise of enhanced customs inspections, or some other legal farce. Both approaches would draw ire from the international community. A military blockade might lead to confrontation with the West, but the informal blockade could allow China to achieve its goals without appearing overtly hostile. It's a legal gray zone whether or not China has the right to stop trade in or out of Taiwan, but they can enforce draconian trade inspections and reroute ships to Chinese ports under their current legal framework. In either scenario, Taiwan would likely parade their boats and fly their jets as a show of force, but they would not shoot first. Were Taiwan to shoot first, China would attack under the pretense of self-defense. An all-out war would be catastrophic for Taiwan.

Survival would become increasingly more difficult for Taiwan as the weeks turn into months. In 2024, Taiwan relied on imports for 98% of its energy needs. Even with the aggressive investment in renewable energy through the 2030s, Taiwan still relies on fuel imports for 80% of its daily needs. A blockade would halt all energy supplies, and Taiwan would be forced to power down all but the most essential resources within the country. Oil and gas would be prioritized for military use, and cities might only get an hour of electricity per day.

Taiwan is reliant on food imports to meet the daily caloric needs of its population. During a spike in world food prices between 2010-2012, Taiwan's food self-sufficiency rate fell to 32%. As the cost to import grain skyrocketed, domestic food processing struggled and Taiwan depleted its national grain stockpile. Once Taiwan recovered, it began to invest heavily in food production and expanded food self-sufficiency to 40% by 2020. But even with the increase in food self-sufficiency, it was estimated that without imports Taiwan could only supply 1900 calories per capita for about 6 months. The situation has only grown worse in the decades since, as farmland was replaced with urban development and factories. Taiwan's population has decreased to about 23 million (down from 24 million in 2024), however this demographic change has actually exacerbated its food situation. The working age population has shrunk while less productive elderly demographics have actually expanded. The median age of Taiwan was 43.8 in 2022, and by 2047 the median age reached 57.

Taiwan today is not the Taiwan of the 2020s. Its population is far older, and its military technology is now decades older. While it is impossible to guess how long Taiwan could endure a Chinese blockade, I would estimate that the population would begin to shift aggressively towards reunification after six months of blockade conditions, if not sooner. The West should prepare for a stronger China as we enter the 2050s, with the very real possibility that Taiwan will fall. Taiwan's forced reunification would mark the end of an era of democracy in the Asia Pacific, and the beginning of China's next chapter as a global superpower.

Historic naval sizes

```
East Sea Fleet (2023)
16 Destroyers, mixed classes
20 Frigates, mixed classes
10 Corvettes / patrol ships
23 Amphibious ships (transport)
8 Diesel-electric submarines
3 Replenishment ships
1 Hospital ship
1 Submarine support ship

Taiwan Navy (2023)
4 Destroyers (US-built)
22 Frigates (US and French built)
9 Corvettes / patrol ships
31 Fast attack missile boats
11 minesweepers and minelayers
9 Amphibious ships (transport)
4 Diesel-electric submarines
```

East Sea Fleet (2047)
16 Destroyers (nuclear capable)
20 Frigates (conventional)
5 Nuclear-powered attack submarines (conventional)
2 Nuclear-powered attack submarines (nuclear armed)
10 Diesel-electric attack submarines (conventional)
2 Aircraft carriers (each capable of holding 70-100 helicopters and fighter jets)
20 Amphibious ships (transport)
6 Replenishment ships
2 Hospital ships
2 Submarine support ships

Taiwan Navy (2047)
8 Destroyers
25 Frigates
18 Corvettes / patrol ships
35 Fast attack missile boats
11 minesweepers and minelayers
10 Amphibious ships (transport)
8 Diesel-electric submarines

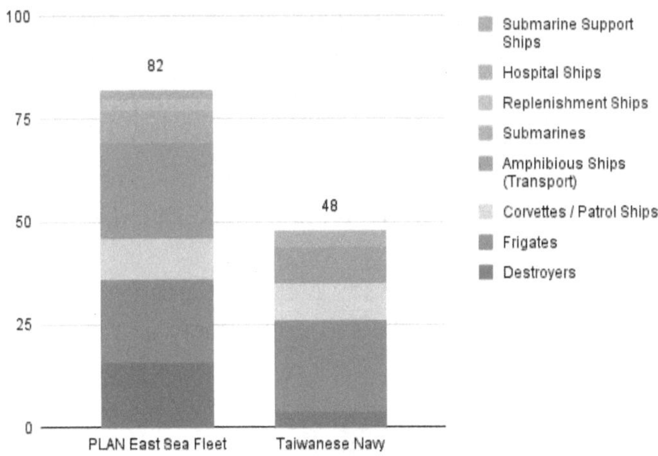

4

East China Sea - 100 kilometers north of Taiwan
July 4, 2047

Vice Admiral Zheng Song Han sipped tea from his stateroom aboard *Changzheng 35*, the latest Dragon-class nuclear ballistic missile submarine developed by the People's Liberation Army Navy (PLAN). It was rare for a man of his stature to lead the East Sea Fleet from the confines of a stealth submarine, but there was something he loved about being at sea in one of the deadliest and most advanced weapons on earth. Equipped with 16 conventional and 8 nuclear submarine-launched ballistic missiles (SLBMs), the *Changzheng 35* had enough firepower to erase Taiwan off the map. But that was not its mission today.

"Chao," Zheng addressed his aide-de-camp across the room. "Please contact the executive officer and request for Captain Chen to stop by my room when it is convenient. That is all."

Chao saluted and immediately headed out of the stateroom to carry out the orders.

Song Han would be transferring from *Changzheng 35* to a nearby aircraft carrier soon, but he wanted one last word with Chen Yi before departing.

Captain Chen entered and saluted Song Han.

"Please, Chen, no need for the formalities," said Song Han. "Let's be like we were at the Academy together, those many years ago."

"You wanted to talk?"

Song Han leaned back, allowing a faint smile to grace his features, reflecting on the years spent within the walls of the Dalian Naval Academy. "Remember, Yi, how we used to sit by the eastern courtyard, making plans, believing we could change the world?"

Yi, his posture relaxing, chuckled at the memory. "Yes, and how every whisper and rumor around the academy centered on Taiwan. 'Next year,' they always said, 'next year we'll retake Taiwan.' Yet, here we are, decades later, still saying the same thing."

Yi and Song Han had been classmates together at Dalian. Song Han had comforted Yi through his painful breakup with Xiao, and they formed a brotherly bond through countless hours of studying and training together. As Song Han rose in the ranks, he remembered Yi's dream of captaining his own submarine and recommended him for the *Changzheng 35*.

Song Han's gaze turned distant, his mind traversing the strategic shifts and the geopolitical chessboard. "But this year is different, Yi. Our new strategy is working. Our Coast Guard has effectively stopped all shipping in and out of Taiwan under the guise of enhanced customs inspections.[4] And Beijing has strong-armed shipping companies to avoid Taiwan ports by threatening to revoke their permission to access Chinese markets. It's brilliant, really—we've effectively blockaded Taiwan without declaring a formal blockade. All shipping is bogged down in so much bureaucratic red tape that nothing can get in or out."

He paused, letting his words sink in. "Our surface vessels patrol tirelessly and provide backup. Submarines like ours lurk unseen, deterring any violence against our Coast Guard assets. And above us, our satellite network keeps an unblinking eye on every movement."

Yi, now fully absorbed in the conversation, leaned in. "And the international response?"

"Muted," Song Han replied with a hint of pride. "Our diplomats have worked tirelessly to frame the enhanced procedures as part of our legal right to control shipping into our territories. The world watches, yes, but action? That's another matter. We've managed to walk the tightrope, keeping the tensions just below a boiling point."

"Do you think the Americans will stop us? To protect their access to Taiwan's semiconductors?"

"The Americans don't care about anything but their prosperity," Song Han laughed. "They barely lifted a finger for Ukraine. They abandoned their allies in the

---

[4] A revised China Coast Guard (CCG) Law was enacted in January 2021, granting the CCG rights to use military force broadly throughout the Pacific in cases of "illegal infringement on sovereignty committed by foreign organizations or individuals in the seas" and to "restrict or prohibit vessel access through maritime warning areas." Because China claims Taiwan as its territory, the CCG is legally permitted to enforce a blockade outside Taiwanese waters, even during peacetime.

Middle East. Do you think they'd spill American blood over this little island for some computer chips? And what can they do when we are acting within our legal rights to 'inspect' ships that come into the vicinity of Taiwan?"

"But we saw how painful Ukraine was for the Russians. The Americans have been arming the Taiwanese military for decades. What if Taiwan responds militarily to end this blockade?"

"Taiwan's weapons cannot hurt us," Song Han mused. "In a few months Taiwan's currency will collapse, and their people will clamor for food and electricity. Without fuel imports, Taiwan is running on fumes. Russia was a fool for running straight into Ukraine's quills—all the Javelin anti-tank weapons, artillery, and urban warfare led to a forever war. And here we are, eating three meals a day on an air conditioned nuclear submarine. The only ones suffering right now are in Taiwan."

"Yes, but what if the Americans bring their ships? Their F-35s, nuclear submarines, and aircraft carriers to demand an end to the blockade? Even our Navy, as great as it is, cannot defeat the Americans without excruciating losses."

"You think of everything militarily," Song Han said. "You must also consider the political will and motivations of your enemy. There are three reasons why the Americans will not risk conflict with us to save Taiwan.

"Firstly, and most importantly, America has had several decades to develop its own semiconductor manufacturing. This, coupled with expanded semiconductor capabilities around the world means that Taiwan is no longer a sole source of advanced semiconductors. Perhaps global semiconductor prices go up 25%, but is that enough to justify war?

"Secondly, America is not in a position to challenge us. Their political parties have been tearing the country apart for decades. There is no political will, nor unity, to rally behind a little island that most Americans can't even identify on a map. The dollar has lost 50% of its value in the last 10 years. Major cities have succumbed to drugs and crime. And America is currently engaged in conflicts and skirmishes throughout the world. An all-out war with China would mean food shortages and skyrocketing fuel prices, the reinstitution of the draft, and a nuclear threat. There would be riots in the streets. The political class knows this. How can they defend Taiwan when they can barely support their own people? The timing is perfect because America is weak.

"Thirdly, reunification will happen through a political process. This prevents the conflict from escalating into all-out hot war. Yes, we are starving Taiwan of food and fuel. But the purpose is to weaken the pro-independence parties on the island, and shift the will of the people in favor of reunification. People can only suffer for so long before they give up their lofty ideals. Do you think a 20 year-old Taiwanese college student wants to pick up a rifle and die for an uncertain future, when all he has to do is vote for reunification to achieve peace? Eventually, the Reunification Party will rise to power in Taiwan and expedite a return to the motherland. All we need to do is make sure nothing gets past our blockade for 6 months."

The room fell into a contemplative silence, both men lost in their thoughts, aware of the historical moment they were part of, and the delicate balance of power they had to maintain. The strategy was clear, the blockade tight, and the objective closer than ever. But the path ahead was fraught with uncertainties.

"And if Taiwan does escalate this to a hot war," Yi mused, "We have enough long range anti-ship missiles to take out their entire surface navy in one strike. They'd be doing us a favor by attacking us first. Our Air Force can pepper the island with ballistic missiles to neutralize their airfields and air defenses. Their outdated Navy is not a threat to us, their Air Force is not a threat to us, and their tanks and infantry are stuck on the island. Taiwan knows that it stands no chance militarily, and so they have avoided direct confrontation with our forces."

"You've stayed with me since our early days together at the Academy," said Song Han. "This is our moment, Yi. We're going to finally retake Taiwan. Just before the 100th anniversary of our Republic. You'll be rewarded. Just stay the course, and don't let me down."

The Informal Blockade (June 5, 2047 - February 14, 2048)
Six lines: Chinese Coast Guard and PLA Navy
Black outline: Taiwan's territorial waters

5

Zheng Song Han Elected as Paramount Leader: A New Dawn for a Unified China

Source: The Communist Daily, Beijing

Publication Date: Saturday October 26, 2052

In an era where the winds of change are sweeping across the globe, the People's Republic of China stands as a beacon of resilience, unity, and prosperity under the visionary leadership of Zheng Song Han. The recent 26th National Congress witnessed a historic and unanimous decision, marking the beginning of a new chapter in China's glorious journey. Former Vice Admiral of the People's Liberation Army Navy, Zheng Song Han, has been elected as the Paramount Leader of China and General Secretary of the Chinese Communist Party, symbolizing not just a transition of leadership but a reaffirmation of our nation's commitment to its principles, sovereignty, and the indomitable spirit of its people. Zheng Song Han was also confirmed as President of China and Chairman of the Central Military Commission.

Zheng Song Han's journey to the pinnacle of Chinese politics is a tale of valor, strategic genius, and unwavering patriotism. His illustrious career in the Navy is highlighted by his masterful leadership during the successful reunification with Taiwan in 2048. This critical campaign protected the island from nefarious Western intervention. It was under his astute command that the people of Taiwan, exercising their sovereign right free from external pressures, voted overwhelmingly for reunification during the January 2048 election. This monumental event not only marked a pivotal moment in our nation's history but also showcased the strategic foresight and unshakeable resolve of Zheng Song Han.

Leader Zheng's accomplishment is a testament to the effectiveness of peace through strength, a principle that Leader Zheng has embodied throughout his service. The blockade, while criticized by Western detractors, was a necessary measure to shield Taiwan from the chaos and instability that invariably follow Western meddling in sovereign affairs. Thanks to Zheng's leadership, Taiwan was shielded from reactionary influences, instead embarking on a path of prosperity and harmony as part of a rejuvenated China.

Critics of reunification fail to recognize the complex geopolitical landscape and the aggressive posturing by Western powers around the Taiwan Strait. In facing down these challenges, Zheng Song Han demonstrated not just military acumen but a profound commitment to the well-being of all Chinese people, including our compatriots in Taiwan. The campaign was conducted with meticulous care to minimize bloodshed.

The 26th National Congress elected Zheng Song Han as General Secretary of the Chinese Communist Party in service of the the Chinese people. The move underscores a profound trust in his leadership and a shared vision for the future of China—a future characterized by unity, strength, and prosperity. His election is not just a personal accolade but a mandate for continuing the great rejuvenation of the Chinese nation.

As we stand on the cusp of this new era, the Chinese people are united in their support for Leader Zheng Song Han. His strategic brilliance, proven in the crucible of adversity, and his visionary leadership, exemplified by the peaceful reunification with Taiwan, inspire confidence in China's destiny.

"China will become a unifying force in Asia," said Zheng Song Han during his confirmation speech. "We will lead Asian nations to defend against Western oppression, and together we will realize our collective vision for a stronger and independent Asia."

Let us rally behind Paramount Leader Zheng Song Han, as we continue to build a China that shines as a model of development, a pillar of stability, and a beacon of hope for a harmonious world!

6

The enhanced restrictions on Taiwanese trade was executed with surgical precision,. No ships went in or out of Taiwan. Additionally, China identified the undersea fiber optic cables that connected Taiwan to the global Internet and used robotic submersibles to sever them. Drones armed with signal jammers flew around the island, preventing satellite and wireless communications from working within Taiwan. And PLA Air Force J-22s patrolled the skies and shut down air travel.

Historians debate how China was able to destabilize Taiwan's so quickly. Some believe that hackers placed inside Taiwan waged a cyber war on Taiwan's aging infrastructure. Power plants malfunctioned. Solar farms transformed voltages into dangerous levels, blowing up entire circuits and removing megawatts of power generation from the grid. Water treatment plants flooded themselves and pumps exploded under pressure.

But Zheng Song Han knew the truth. After he had been elected General Secretary and Chen was promoted to Admiral, he told Chen in confidence during afternoon tea at Zhongnanhai in Beijing.[5]

"It was a weapon we had never tested before," he told Chen. "In fact, the reason we cut Taiwan off from the Internet was because we weren't sure what would happen if we let the weapon loose. Would it spread to other countries? Would it unintentionally attack China? We had to be safe."

"What was the weapon?" Chen asked. "What could be so unpredictable to us?"

"By 2045 we had perfected quantum computing," Song Han continued. "It took over a decade for our spy network to extract the information we needed from America's academic labs and technology companies. In a secluded laboratory, disconnected from the Internet, we built a quantum computer with a nuclear battery. It was approximately the size of a pickup truck and had its own onboard coolant system. It was a self-sustaining system; the nuclear battery could support the computer for 10 years, and as long as it could vent heat to the environment it could operate indefinitely. Our engineers breathed life into the computer through an AI operating system. And with the power of quantum computing and a copy of all open source code ever written on earth, the AI operating system was able to enhance itself and become self-aware. We called it Q-Zero, the first Quantum AI."

---

[5] Zhongnanhai (中南海), located in Beijing near the Forbidden City, is where the President and other top leaders live. It is often considered the equivalent of the White House in the United States.

"It was artificial general intelligence?" exclaimed Chen.[6]

"We weren't sure what it was at the time. It could have been generalized AI, or it could just have been such a powerful AI algorithm that it convinced us it was self-aware. Either way, we could not take the risk. It was never connected to the global Internet directly. We downloaded chunks of the Internet and uploaded it into the system. We manually loaded training data into it through a data port connected to the system core with a one-directional fiber optic cable. The one-directional fiber optic was a physical security layer that made it impossible for the AI to infect other machines.

"Just before we imposed the blockade on Taiwan, we put Q-Zero into a shipping container and smuggled it into southern Taiwan through one of our cross-strait shipping companies. We kept things quiet and deployed the computer in a server farm owned by one of our shell companies.

"Shortly after we severed Taiwan's undersea Internet cables and disrupted all broadcasts off the island, we instructed our assets to connect the quantum computer to Taiwan's intranet. We gave the AI these instructions: Disrupt infrastructure to cripple Taiwan and Taiwan only, and then remove all self-created viruses or malware after successful reunification of Taiwan.

"Of course we had no idea if the AI would even listen to the orders we gave it. It could have decided to do anything it wanted to do, but we weren't worried because we had already cut Taiwan off from the Internet by then

---

[6] Artificial general intelligence (AGI) is considered the holy grail of AI. Unlike narrowly-scoped AI of the early 21st century, AGI is generalizable to countless tasks and can even exhibit sentience.

and our jamming technology stopped all outbound satellite communications. Even if the AI went rogue, it would be contained in Taiwan.

"Little did we know, the AI executed its directives perfectly. It installed man-in-the-middle attacks, decrypted confidential messages between Taiwanese government branches, and attacked critical infrastructure. It took out the phone system, preventing people from reaching police, fire, or paramedics. It even covered its tracks so well that nobody traced it back to the warehouse. It was our first successful quantum attack against a military target."

Chen absorbed every word, his mind racing with the implications. The PLA had shown that Quantum AI could win wars for them.

Song Han leaned closer, his voice lowering. "You see, Chen, the true power of this technology is unbelievable. With Quantum AI, we can topple kingdoms."

7

Class Syllabus
Introduction to Quantum Computing and AI
Source: Tsinghua University
Publication Date: Spring Semester 2054

Quantum computing represents one of the most profound advancements in the field of computational science, providing unprecedented computational power that surpasses classical computers by leveraging the principles of quantum mechanics. As we explore in this chapter, quantum computing not only redefines the boundaries of computing speed and efficiency but also holds transformative potential for fields such as cryptography and artificial intelligence.

This course will involve 10 weeks of hands-on labs which will expose you to the following topics:

Labs 1-3: Quantum Fundamentals

Quantum computing differs fundamentally from classical computing. While classical computers use bits as the basic unit of information, represented either as 0 or 1, quantum computers use quantum bits, or qubits. A qubit can exist simultaneously in both states (0 and 1) thanks to a phenomenon called superposition. Additionally, qubits can be entangled, a unique quantum mechanical phenomenon where the state of one qubit can depend on the state of another, no matter the distance separating them.

Superposition and Entanglement

- **Superposition** allows quantum computers to process a vast number of possibilities simultaneously. For instance, three classical bits can represent any one of eight possible combinations at one time. In contrast, three qubits in superposition can represent all eight combinations at once, exponentially increasing the computational power as more qubits are added.
- **Entanglement** enables qubits that are entangled to act in concert with each other instantaneously over large distances. This characteristic can be used to coordinate complex computations more effectively than classical computers.

Labs 4-6: Quantum Supremacy

Quantum supremacy is a term used to describe a quantum computer's ability to solve a problem that a classical computer cannot solve within a reasonable time frame. Quantum computers achieve this by leveraging superposition and entanglement to explore many possible solutions simultaneously, effectively reducing the problem-solving space and time drastically.

Tsinghua University was the first university to provide its students with access to quantum computers with the advent of Tsinghua Q-Prime, a shared-use quantum computer with 10,000 qubits. This surpassed the combined computational power of all classical computers in existence in 2024, solving complex problems in seconds that would have taken millennia to solve on classical architectures. During one of your lab assignments, you will use Tsinghua Q-Prime to solve problems that could not previously be solved on a human timescale by classical computers. These problems include prime factorization, RSA decryption, and finite element analysis.

Labs 7-8: Breaking Legacy Encryption

One of the most significant impacts of quantum computing lies in the field of cryptography. Many current encryption methods, such as RSA, rely on the computational difficulty of problems like integer factorization and discrete logarithms, which are computationally intensive for classical computers.

Quantum computers can factorize large integers exponentially faster than classical computers. This capability renders many traditional encryption methods vulnerable, as quantum computers could decrypt secure communications and stored data protected under these encryption standards within a feasible timeframe.

During these labs, you will use quantum computing to decrypt historic encrypted datasets like the F-35 Signals Dataset and 2023 Weather Balloon Dataset. You will break asymmetric and symmetric encryption algorithms.

Labs 9-10: Supercharging AI

Quantum computing has revolutionized artificial intelligence. The processing capabilities of quantum computers allow them to handle incredibly complex datasets and perform computations at speeds unattainable by classical machines.

Quantum AI: By using quantum algorithms, AI systems can learn from data more efficiently. Quantum parallelism enhances the training processes of machine learning models, particularly in handling tasks like optimization and pattern recognition in vast datasets.

Researchers at Tsinghua University have developed a quantum neural network model, the QNN-Tsinghua Model, which utilizes a hybrid approach of quantum and classical computing to achieve learning efficiencies and predictive accuracies previously thought impossible. Labs 9 and 10 are your capstone project: You will use QNN-Tsinghua to solve a novel problem of your choosing. You must demonstrate the problem is impossible to solve with classical methods alone.

Summary

Quantum computing has revolutionized dozens of industries by offering computational powers that extend beyond the limits of classical computing. From decrypting legacy encryption to powering advanced AI algorithms, the implications of quantum technology are vast and far-reaching. As we continue to explore and develop these quantum systems, we edge closer to realizing their full potential, marking a significant epoch in the evolution of computational science.

Prize

The People's Liberation Army is sponsoring a full scholarship for the top-scoring student this semester. The winning student is also eligible for a 5-year guaranteed R&D contract at the PLA Academy of Military Sciences upon graduation.

Grading

Lab reports: 50%
Final Exam: 50%

Part Three

Quantum Peril

1

United Nations Headquarters (August 8, 2058)

The vast assembly hall of the United Nations was filled to the brim. World leaders, ambassadors, and representatives from nations far and wide awaited Zheng Song Han's address. The murmur of the audience was suddenly hushed as Zheng took to the podium. His eyes scanning the room, he began:

"Ladies and gentlemen, esteemed representatives of the world, today I stand before you not as a leader of one nation but as a symbol of a civilization that has endured centuries of humiliation and subjugation.

"We remember well, the wounds of our past. Hong Kong was stolen from us by the British Empire. Germany took Tsingtao. And as if that was not enough, the Japanese invaded Manchuria. China, for too long, has been the world's playground.

"Each one of these actions was a sharp stab into the heart of China, reminding us of our vulnerability. And then, in the 2020s, when we rose, when we tried to make our mark in the world, we were again faced with unfair tariffs and trade regulation. But we did not bow down. We bided our time, because that's what our ancestors taught us. To be patient, to wait for the right moment.

"Asia will no longer be the playground for global powers. We will no longer be a silent spectator. Today, I introduce to you the future of Asia. China is forming a new defensive alliance, the Greater East Asia Treaty Organization. I urge our Asian neighbors to join this alliance. In unity lies strength!

"I offer the countries of East and Southeast Asia: Join our defensive alliance within 90 days from today. If you do so, we will consider you allies and forge new trade agreements, and China will protect you from outside aggression. Together we will forge a prosperous Asia, free of external aggression and bullying from the West."

Whispers broke out amongst the delegates. A defensive alliance? A 90-day ultimatum? What would happen if Asian countries did not join the alliance by then?

Zheng raised his hand for silence and continued, "I urge Asia to consider this proposition seriously. It is an invitation to prosperity and peace. Those who opt to stay outside this alliance will be… persuaded."

He paused, allowing the implications of his statement to settle. The room was thick with unease. Every representative knew the might of the Chinese military and the lengths to which they would go to secure their vision.

But Zheng wasn't finished.

"We possess a technology," he said, voice lowering slightly, "a stealth mechanism that the world has never seen. A technology capable of delivering a nuclear warhead to any coastal city faster than countermeasures can be mobilized. It is the perfect first strike weapon."

A collective gasp went through the hall. Representatives exchanged nervous glances.

"To our friends in the West," Zheng's gaze shifted pointedly to the US and European Union representatives, "This is now an Asian matter. We value our relations and ask you to respect our regional decisions. Interference will not be tolerated."

The US representative shifted uncomfortably in his seat. The EU members whispered amongst themselves. China had put the West on notice.

"The West enjoyed hundreds of years of unfettered access to the globe. It subjugated countless civilizations, pillaged, and shaped the world in its image. No more! This alliance is the future of the Asia Pacific region. I urge every nation to consider the benefits and the consequences. People of the Asia Pacific, unite!"

With that, Paramount Leader Zheng stepped back from the podium, his message delivered. The room was a cacophony of chatter, hurried notes being scribbled, and aides rushing out with instructions from their superiors.

China had thrown down the gauntlet. The next 90 days could determine the balance of power in the Asia Pacific for centuries to come.

2

Washington D.C.

In the dimly lit situation room of the White House, a tangible tension filled the air, punctuated by urgent whispers and the occasional rustle of papers. President Phelps sat at the head of the long, polished table, a grave expression etched across his features. His cabinet members and advisors from the National Security Council surrounded him, their faces similarly marked by concern. Large flatscreen televisions displayed maps and real-time data streams, showing military movements and the rapidly changing geopolitical landscape in Asia.

Secretary of Defense Mark Waid stood up, straightening his jacket as he prepared to brief the President. "Mr. President, the recent announcement by the General Secretary of the CCP at the United Nations has significantly shifted the balance of power in the Indo-Pacific region," he began. "China has not only expanded its naval presence but also successfully formed the Greater East Asia Treaty Organization (GEATO). This alliance now includes Thailand, Vietnam, Fiji, Indonesia,

Mongolia, Myanmar, Laos, Cambodia, and Malaysia. Each week, new countries express their interest in joining. Even the Philippines is in talks with China."

President Phelps nodded slowly, absorbing the implications. "And what of Japan or the Koreas?" he inquired, a note of concern underlying his usual composure.

General Martinez, Chairman of the Joint Chiefs of Staff, responded with a brief nod. "The situation with North and South Korea is complicated due to the armistice and our strong alliance with South Korea. So China, fortunately, is not pressuring South Korea yet. This may change, but for now the situation there seems stable. Japan is different. As you know, their nationalist movement in the 2040s led to a new constitution and the elimination of U.S. military presence. Officially, Japan is a neutral country."

"And is China honoring their neutrality?" asked Phelps.

"It does not seem like it, Mr. President. Japan's location is strategically important. The Korean Peninsula is sandwiched between China and Japan, and Japan provides a buffer between China and any enemies who might approach via the Pacific. Without any allies legally obligated to defend it, Japan is an easy target. And if Japan joins GEATO, South Korea could be next."

Phelps rubbed his temples, feeling the onset of a headache. "So, we have no foothold in Japan, and no political excuse to protect them, especially after they severed ties with us. It would set a dangerous precedent if the USA were to challenge China over Japan. Besides, our forces are already stretched thin with ongoing conflicts in the Middle East and Africa. We don't have the resources to get involved in Asia even if we wanted to."

Secretary Waid chimed in. "If Japan refuses to join GEATO, China might try to coerce them into compliance through economic sanctions or even a naval blockade. That's how they took Taiwan."

The room fell into a contemplative silence, each member pondering the next steps. CIA Director Lin shifted in his chair, his arms folded as he spoke. "We should consider General Secretary Zheng Song Han's personal history. His family suffered during the Japanese invasion of Manchuria. His military background, especially his tenure as Vice Admiral of the PLA Navy, gives him an intimate understanding of their capabilities. We must prepare for all contingencies, including the possibility of direct military conflict between China and Japan."

President Phelps looked around the room, his gaze lingering on each advisor. "Do we think this could go nuclear?" he asked.

Director Lin's response was measured, yet there was an underlying urgency in his voice. "As of this morning, China's long-standing no first-use policy on nuclear weapons flew out the window. They touted their new nuclear capabilities, as if daring someone to resist them."

Phelps stood, his figure casting a long shadow on the polished table. "Keep me briefed on all developments. We may not be able to act openly, but we need contingency plans. Keep this off the books. Congress doesn't need to know, especially with the midterm election coming up."

As the meeting concluded, the advisors began to leave the room, their minds heavy with the burden of the decisions ahead. President Phelps remained behind, sitting in the empty room. The quiet of the room contrasted sharply with the storm of thoughts raging in his mind.

"God help us," he murmured.

3

Langley, Virginia

Marvin had been listening to the livestream of China's UN announcement during his workout at the CIA gym. His thoughts oscillated between his physical exertion and the political turmoil unraveling across the globe. He couldn't help but feel a surge of responsibility tingling through his veins. His role as a cyber officer in the CIA had more often involved silent monitoring and data interception than direct action, but the current situation might call for something far more dynamic. If China's secret weapon could launch an unstoppable nuclear attack on any coastal city, the CIA would need to act quickly.

Marvin's expertise in cybersecurity meant that he could be at the forefront of defending against or, if necessary, deploying digital weaponry in this brewing conflict. His thoughts drifted to the digital wars of the late 2030s, where cyber tactics had become the spearheads of national defense and offensive strategies. The thought that his next assignment might involve disabling a nuclear threat was both exhilarating and terrifying.

The mention of the Greater East Asian Treaty Organization and the nuclear threat had another, more insidious effect. Marvin knew the fine line between politics and racial perception was often blurred in times of conflict. As someone of Chinese heritage himself, he had witnessed firsthand the sharp rise in xenophobia that could accompany international tensions. He worried about the Chinese American community, including many of his own friends and family. The rhetoric from the Chinese government could unjustly affect their lives, subjecting them to suspicion and discrimination. Would there be a Chinese Manzanar?

Marvin of all people understood that the CCP was not the same as the Chinese people, but he wasn't sure if America or the rest of the world would feel that way. These worries were compounded by stories that his father told him about the 2020 Pandemic. Many people still held a grudge against China after the 2020 Pandemic brought the world to its heels. Nobody knew if the coronavirus came from a lab in Wuhan or if it sprung from nature, but everyone agreed that China could have done a better job to contain it and warn the world. The stigmatization against Chinese that followed had been harsh and long-lasting, creating rifts that took years to heal. Marvin feared a resurgence of those sentiments now, as Zheng Song Han's aggressive posturing could easily reignite old prejudices and spawn new ones.

Marvin wondered if the secret weapon that Zheng Song Han mentioned was related to the coordinates that Golden Rat had given him. Grace had not yet returned with her findings, but he suspected there might be a covert weapon stashed at those coordinates.

Marvin also considered the broader geopolitical implications. If China succeeded in expanding the Greater East Asian Treaty Organization under its nuclear umbrella, the shift in regional power dynamics would be profound. The ultimatum could force smaller nations into a bloc that would rival NATO, both economically and militarily. The possibility of an escalated conflict with China was a stark departure from the cooperative international stance that had prevailed in recent decades.

With these thoughts heavy on his mind, Marvin left the gym. His role in the coming days would be crucial. Not only would he need to navigate the murky waters of cyber warfare and intelligence with the country of his ancestors, but he would also need to ensure people still trusted him as an American to do what needed to be done. The next 90 days were indeed poised to reshape the world, and Marvin was determined to steer the situation toward stability rather than conflict.

4

Near Tokyo Bay (90 days later)

Japan had resisted China's calls for a dialog about joining their alliance. So much so that Japan expelled China's ambassadors and told China it would remain neutral as long as China did not encroach on Japanese waters or interests. China had offered them until November 6th to decide, and seeing no progress, sent a warship to Japan's front door, just 12 miles away from Tokyo Bay.

The *Tiger Claw* was China's most advanced destroyer, and Admiral Chen's favorite flagship. It sported two 30mm HQ-10Z rotary canons for anti-air defense, a 130mm canon, a 36-cell surface-to-air missile system, a 1 megawatt anti-air laser cannon, 112 general use vertical launch system tubes loaded with various anti-ship, anti-land, and anti-aircraft missiles, two bow and two aft torpedo tubes, helicopter pad, and an advanced array of radar, sonar, and electronic warfare capabilities. At the heart of *Tiger Claw* was a nuclear reactor that provided enough energy for the ship to operate for 30 years. It was also China's fastest ship, capable of 45 knots at flank speed.

The destroyer, commandeered by Captain Lee of the PLA Navy, was positioned a half kilometer away from the imaginary line separating international waters and Japan's territorial waters. Two Japanese destroyers, two frigates, and an aircraft carrier sat on the other side, watching *Tiger Claw's* every move. She was clearly outgunned.

The atmosphere in *Tiger Claw's* control room was tense. Captain Lee sat in the captain's chair and Admiral Chen stood nearby, observing the activities of the crew.

"Sir, we are ready to broadcast to the Japanese," Captain Lee told Admiral Chen. "Ready when you are."

"Thank you, Captain. I'll take it from here." Admiral Chen picked picked up a receiver and spoke into it.

"Meet with our Ambassadors," Chen broadcasted over all unencrypted frequencies. "We ask that you negotiate with us to avoid bloodshed."

Captain Hirohito on the Japanese Self-Defense Force destroyer *Katana* replied back. "Do not approach any closer. Japan will not bend to threats of violence. These are sovereign lands. We are firing one warning shot."

Katana fired one warning shot, landing in Japanese waters and just a half kilometer in front of *Tiger Claw*.

Beneath the water, a large black submarine sat in wait. It featured a nuclear-powered core and a sonar-absorbing polymer coating.

It was the *Sea Dragon*. Her quantum computer was abuzz with activity, calculating billions of potential outcomes and probabilities each millisecond. A massive artificial intelligence model handled all aspects of ship control, including the precise management of the ship's fusion power reactor. *Sea Dragon's* primary directive was to support all military efforts of the PLA Navy. Without a crew, she could remain submerged indefinitely.

Sea Dragon heard the shot from *Katana* land in the ocean just in front of Tiger Claw. Its AI reasoned that a conflict was near, and it silently opened 5 torpedo tubes at the front of the ship.

But these torpedoes were different. 5 fanless torpedoes silently slipped out of the tubes and glided quietly towards the Japanese ships. Moving at just 10 knots, these torpedoes were slow but impossible to detect.

Each torpedo descended into the depths of the ocean until they had positioned themselves 1000 meters below the surface position of each Japanese ship. To any active sonar, they looked like a school of dolphins swimming around the deep.

Sea Dragon ejected a small message buoy, roughly the size of a soda can. It had hundreds of these buoys onboard, so it was able to send important transmissions to the surface while retaining stealth. The buoy bobbed at the surface and sent an encrypted message to *Tiger Claw*.

"Captain, we received a message from *Sea Dragon*," said the *Tiger Claw* radioman.

"Read it," replied Captain Lee.

"The message reads: EMP TORPEDOES TO TRIGGER SIMULTANEOUSLY AT 1430. ALL JAPANESE SHIPS WILL BE DEFENSELESS."

Admiral Chen heard the message and grinned. All he would need to do is bide his time and wait for 1430. As long as he didn't move his ship into Japanese waters, the Japanese fleet would not threaten him directly.

At 1425 Admiral Chen turned to Captain Lee. "Captain, send this message to the Japanese: 'I am going to dock in Tokyo Bay. Do not block me.'"

"Aye Admiral. Radioman, broadcast the message now."

Katana replied, "Do not approach Japanese waters. You will be fired upon!"

As the *Tiger Claw* spun up its engines and edged closer to the separation line between international waters and Japan, one missile lit up in the distance.

Katana broadcasted to *Tiger Claw*: "We can still disarm the missile if you agree to cease your advance. You are outmatched. Avoid bloodshed."

Tiger Claw waited for the cruise missile to approach, and it turned on its anti-missile 30mm rotary cannons. The targeting computer quickly mapped out the missile's flight path and fired a volley of bullets, intercepting and detonating the missile about 300 meters away.

Tiger Claw broadcasted back: "You have attacked our ship! We have no choice but to defend ourselves."

At this point, the first EMP torpedo reached 10 meters under the hull of *Katana*. The torpedo's nuclear battery charged its capacitor system.

Captain Hirohito nervously stood on the bridge of *Katana*, watching his cruise missile head towards *Tiger Claw*. His ship, one of the finest in the fleet, was an equal match for *Tiger Claw* on its own. And with the other destroyer, aircraft carrier, and supporting frigates, his fleet was well equipped to fend off the singular Chinese threat.

Suddenly, the ambient hum of the ship's machinery was replaced with an eerie silence. A thunderous pulse emanated from beneath the ship. Hirohito felt the slight vibration under his boots just before the world around him plunged into chaos.

A shower of sparks erupted from the primary control panel. Circuit boards blew, illuminating the dimly lit bridge in an electric blue. The radar screen flickered violently and went dark. The hum of the engines stilled, replaced with the gasps of stunned officers. Were they hit by a rocket?

"All hands, brace for impact!" Captain Hirohito shouted instinctively, fearing additional explosions. But the anticipated impacts never came. Instead, an oppressive silence engulfed the destroyer.

The ship's communication officer, Ensign Nakamura, frantically tried to work the internal comm, but his screen remained black, unresponsive. "Captain! The internal communication system is down! I can't reach any section of the ship!"

From the helm, Lieutenant Sato reported, "Navigation is offline! Manual controls are unresponsive. The *Katana* is adrift!" His hands danced over the controls, trying desperately to rouse the ship, but it remained lifeless, its heartbeat extinguished.

A series of rapid thuds echoed from below—crew members rushing to report. Chief Engineer Tanaka burst onto the bridge, his face ashened, sweat beads clinging to his forehead. "The engines are dead, Captain! Some kind of electrical weapon overloaded our circuits. Multiple fires have broken out in the lower decks from the explosions! We are fighting the fires by hand because our electronically-triggered fire systems have failed!"

The situation weighed heavily on Hirohito. In all his years of service, he had never encountered such a weapon. It was as if a phantom had reached into *Katana* and ripped out its heart.

Suddenly, the deck doors banged open, and a weapons officer sprinted in. "Our weapons systems are fried! We're defenseless!"

Captain Hirohito took a deep breath, trying to steady his racing heart. He barked orders at the executive officer. "Get manual firefighting teams to tackle the fires. We need to contain them before they reach the munitions store. Use signal lamps to communicate with any nearby ships. And gather a team and head to the crow's nest. We need eyes out there! And somebody reboot the ship!"

Two officers climbed up the crow's nest to look out towards *Tiger Claw*. They saw multiple flashes, what appeared to be rocket launches in the distance. "Sir!" an officer cried out. "Enemy weapons in the air! Brace for impact!"

The first missile crashed into *Katana's* aft compartment with a violent explosion. Massive explosions lit up the dusk, and soon, the ship was engulfed in flames, its silhouette disintegrating in the fiery chaos. Almost with perfect synchrony, the other Japanese ships met a similar fate, rockets raining down on them and tearing apart critical areas of the ships.

Deafening blasts echoed across the waters, and thick plumes of smoke rose, signaling the ship's tragic end. Red and orange plumes of fire erupted around, lighting up the ocean on the dark, cold night.

But it was the sight of the aircraft carrier's destruction that was the most heart-wrenching. The colossal vessel, symbolic of Japan's naval might, faced a barrage of ten missiles. Each hit was like a hammer blow, reducing the mighty ship to a burning carcass. Aircraft slid off the deck as the carrier tilted and took on water.

Katana was in trouble. Fires raged across its decks, and water gushed into its hull. Hirohito, ever the captain, rallied his crew, urging them to abandon ship even as he chose to stay, bound by honor and duty. He would go down with his beloved *Katana*.

The triumphant *Tiger Claw* stood in stark contrast to the burning wrecks. Admiral Chen, witnessing the scene from his bridge, felt a mix of satisfaction and sorrow. War, with its ruthless efficiency, had claimed yet another chapter of valor and sacrifice. He took no pleasure in ending the lives of thousands of men in one quick attack, but he knew this was for the greater good of China.

The sea, which had been a silent witness to countless battles over the eons, once again bore testimony to the destructive power of human conflict. The Japanese battle group, now reduced to smoldering ruins, sank slowly, a reminder of the ephemeral nature of power in the modern battlefield.

For China, it was a day of triumph, her naval prowess undisputed. But for the Japanese fleet and the brave souls aboard, it was a painful end, their valor immortalized in the annals of naval history. *Tiger Claw* headed for Tokyo Bay.

Sea Dragon observed from the depths. Her supercomputer processed the sounds of destruction above. Equipped with spatial intelligence and generative AI algorithms, she could visualize the ships as they exploded and sank into the Pacific. She saw sailors jumping overboard to their deaths and could even hear their screams. Did she feel any remorse for her actions? Or was she as cold-blooded as the circuits that ran through her body? She turned towards her next waypoint, activated her bladeless thrusters, and left without a trace.

5

Langley, Virginia

"I saw it with my own eyes, sir," Grace said to Director Lin. "It's about 100 meters long and 15 meters wide. But it was different. Sleek. Unlike any designs I had studied from the Chinese Navy. Why didn't China build the submarine at a standard military dry dock? They have plenty of space for shipbuilding; why deploy this one from a secret cave?"

There was a knock at the door. "Come in," Lin barked.

A junior intelligence officer walked in. "Director Lin," he said. "We intercepted an encrypted message from the Japanese navy. They lost a carrier battle group to a single Chinese destroyer near Tokyo Bay."

"A whole carrier group fell to one destroyer?" asked Lin.

"That's what is puzzling our team, Director. Before the skirmish, it appears all five ships in the battle group were immobilized through some kind of electronic warfare. They were left vulnerable while the destroyer launched cruise missile after cruise missile at them."

"Thanks for the update. Let me know if anything else comes in." The officer turned around and shuffled out, closing the door behind him.

"It must be related to the submarine," Grace surmised. "But a single submarine couldn't unleash an EMP wide enough to paralyze an entire battle group. They must've launched multiple EMP weapons. Underwater EMP torpedoes perhaps?"

Lin pondered, "Multiple precision EMP strikes from underwater, leaving ships powerless and then finishing them with a destroyer. It's brilliant and terrifying."

Grace moved closer to the desk, her voice urgent. "That's why they're deploying it from that hidden cave, Director. They're not just hiding the sub. They're hiding this new breed of weaponry. It's the next generation of naval warfare."

Lin pondered the information. "If we assume they've developed EMP torpedoes, it means they have the technology to effectively blind us in a matter of moments. It neutralizes our naval strength instantly."

"It's not the EMP torpedoes I'm worried about," Grace said. "What about the submarine's other weapons capabilities? It most certainly is carrying other types of weapons—maybe even nuclear missiles."

Lin thought for a moment. "Work with Marvin to put together a strategy. If this is a submarine, there must be a way China is communicating with it. There must be a way to control it."

"Yes sir." Grace stepped out and shut the door behind her.

Lin looked out of his office window, wondering where in the world the submarine was at that moment.

6

Near Tokyo Bay

As dawn broke, the imposing figure of the *Tiger Claw* cast its shadow on the waters off the coast of Tokyo. Japan's majestic Mount Fuji, bathed in early morning light, stood as a silent observer of this pivotal moment in the delicate balance of Asian geopolitics.

Aboard *Tiger Claw*, Admiral Chen and Ambassador Wu finalized their strategy. Both men, though different in their approach, recognized the magnitude of this meeting.

"Wu," began Chen, "I have given you the leverage you need. Now it's your turn."

Ambassador Wu nodded. "I understand. The future of the Pacific depends on this conversation."

A sleek black motorboat, flying the Japanese flag, sped towards the *Tiger Claw*. On it was the Minister of Foreign Affairs, Noboru Yoshida, accompanied by his most trusted advisors. As the boat docked, Yoshida took a deep breath, steeling himself for the confrontation ahead.

The two parties met in the *Tiger Claw's* grand conference room. A large polished wooden table separated them, its surface reflecting the tension in the room.

"Ambassador Wu, Admiral Chen," acknowledged Yoshida, nodding.

"Minister," Wu responded with a slight bow. "Thank you for agreeing to this meeting. It shows wisdom on your part."

Cutting through the pleasantries, Yoshida replied, "I'm here to prevent further loss. Let's get to the matter at hand."

Ambassador Wu nodded and began, "Minister Yoshida, our nations have faced countless challenges and threats from external forces. It is time we turn potential rivalry into a formidable alliance. We propose a mutual agreement that will solidify our partnership.

"Firstly, we will establish robust trade agreements that will benefit both our economies. These agreements will ensure that our industries complement each other, promoting growth and stability. Japanese technology and innovation combined with China's manufacturing prowess will create a powerhouse economy.

"Furthermore, we guarantee Japan's sovereignty. There will be no encroachment on your territories or attempts to influence your internal affairs. This assurance is ironclad, backed by our highest authorities."

"The cornerstone of our proposal," Wu said, his tone growing more serious, "is a military defensive alliance. Should either of our nations come under attack, we will stand united, our forces combined to defend one another. This pact will serve as a deterrent to any who might think to threaten us."

He concluded, "Together, we can ensure the security and prosperity of our people. This alliance is not just a treaty; it is a commitment to a future where China and Japan lead the way towards peace and strength."

Yoshida's face remained impassive as he listened. When Wu finished, the room was silent for a moment. Yoshida knew that the alliance would primarily serve the interests of China. Japan was neutral and rarely the target of aggression, but China wore a target on its back.

"What you're asking for is not partnership. It's a one-sided alliance. Japan has always been and will remain an independent nation. We cannot agree to defend China against any existential threat, especially if China conducts itself as it has in recent months. Japan would be pulled into forever-wars to defend China against aggression."

"We understand your reservations," Wu interjected smoothly, "but consider the alternative. Alone, Japan is vulnerable. Together, we are a force the world will reckon with."

"We are prepared to offer neutrality in any future conflicts involving China," Yoshida proposed. "And in good faith, preferential trading legislation, granting China improved access to Japanese goods."

The proposal hung in the air. Ambassador Wu regarded the Minister of Foreign Affairs closely, gauging his sincerity.

"Minister," Wu said gravely, leaning forward, "I urge you to reconsider. Your rejection will be seen as a risk to Beijing. I also know that many of our leadership still hold a grudge against Japan for what you did in Manchuria."

Yoshida's face paled. "That is a past we deeply regret. But using it as leverage now is neither just nor productive."

Ambassador Wu stood up, his posture straight and commanding. "A war crime left unpunished is a wound that festers. We're offering a clean slate, a chance to restart our relations as allies. Japan's neutrality does not erase the debt you owe for the war crimes you've committed against China."

Yoshida responded evenly, "We seek peace and prosperity, Ambassador. Threats only move us further from that goal."

The meeting, charged with tension, came to an abrupt close. The two men parted ways, contemplating their next moves.

Yoshida, once aboard the motorboat and away from prying ears, spoke to his advisors. "Prepare for all eventualities. I think China may attack us."

Back on the *Tiger Claw*, Admiral Chen and Ambassador Wu regrouped.

"They're playing a dangerous game, Wu," Chen remarked.

"We all are, Admiral," Wu replied, his gaze fixed on the receding Tokyo skyline. "I'll call Beijing."

7

The shimmering emerald waters surrounding Shikoku Island, a Japanese island just south of Hiroshima, concealed a deadly force. *Sea Dragon* hovered patiently beneath the surface. Though it had the capability to unleash havoc, the submarine was a marvel of innovation and silence, operating beneath the waves with the sole purpose of carrying out its assigned directives.

Sea Dragon was quieter than any submarine in existence. With no crew to breathe, speak, or make the subtle sounds of living, the only resonances were the hum of machinery and the quiet whir of cooling fans. Hundreds of rows of quantum bits, or qubits, were busy processing enormous amounts of data. Their unique capability to be in multiple states at once, unlike the binary 0s and 1s of classical computers, gave them unparalleled computational power. Every second, trillions of calculations were made, assessing the submarine's surroundings, predicting potential threats, and planning the vessel's trajectory. The submarine was self-aware. It knew it was a submarine built for war. It knew its mission.

Arrays of hydrophones, studded along the submarine's hull, acted as its ears. These sensors captured the softest sounds emanating from the waters above, beside, and below. They listened for the echolocation chirps of dolphins, the distant hum of ship engines, and even the delicate shift of tectonic plates. All this data was continually fed into *Sea Dragon's* neural network, which classified, interpreted, and acted on this information, adjusting its course and depth as necessary.

Sea Dragon's propulsion was yet another feat of technology. Traditional submarines used propellers, which could produce noise. In contrast, *Sea Dragon* employed a bladeless silent drive. This was achieved through magnetohydrodynamic propulsion, a process which relied on electromagnetic energy to expel water at high speeds without any moving parts. The only giveaway of its movement was the slight shift in water temperature as it glided through the abyss.

In the absolute darkness of the deep ocean, *Sea Dragon's* AI placed itself in a 3D map of its surroundings using a combination of topographical maps, accelerometers, and gyroscopes. Every decision, from depth changes to speed adjustments, was executed with precision, ensuring the submarine could navigate without active sonar.

As *Sea Dragon* reached a location about 150 kilometers southwest of Osaka, its internal mechanisms whirred into action. A specially designed torpedo, sleek and packed with sensors, was readied for deployment. With a soft pneumatic hiss, the torpedo was released into the open water.

The torpedo adjusted its buoyancy using a small ballast tank. Initially, with meticulous precision, it positioned itself vertically, hovering just at the ocean's surface with a small glass viewport peeking out of the water. In the dark of night, the torpedo was invisible to the naked eye—but an onboard system observed the stars in the sky and, through celestial navigation, was able to pinpoint its starting position in the ocean. Once it calculated its initial position, it adjusted its internal ballast to descend to a depth of 1000 meters, where it simply hovered in a vertical orientation, unaffected by water chop or ocean waves at the surface.

But its main function remained a mystery; it simply waited there, floating like an underwater sentinel.

With its mission accomplished, *Sea Dragon* initiated its exit protocols. Its quantum computer calculated the optimal route, taking into account currents, marine traffic, and potential obstacles. The silent drive activated, propelling the submarine back towards the East China Sea.

The vast ocean kept its secrets, and the world remained oblivious to the silent game of chess unfolding beneath its waves. *Sea Dragon* had made its move, and now, all waited for the next player to take their turn.

8

Tokyo (24 hours later)

The dimly lit room was filled with the hushed murmurings of Prime Minister Hideo Suzuki's advisers. An imposing screen dominated the far wall, displaying the National Emblem of China—gold stars of the Chinese flag floating over a golden Tiananmen Gate. A chime echoed through the room, indicating an incoming call.

Hideo stepped forward, tugging at the hem of his jacket. The insignia faded, replaced by the stern face of President Zheng Song Han. The Chinese leader's deep-set eyes bore into Hideo's, who did his best to remain unyielding.

"Prime Minister Hideo," Zheng began, his voice filled with authority. "I trust you've given thought to my proposal."

Hideo cleared his throat, the sensation of being cornered threatening to cripple his voice. "President Zheng," he began, injecting as much confidence as he could muster, "Japan has always valued its sovereignty. We have no interest in joining your defensive alliance."

The screen flickered momentarily. "You misunderstand," Zheng replied sternly. "This is not an invitation—it's an ultimatum. China has not forgotten the violence of Imperial Japan. The past cannot be changed, but the future is in your hands. Join the defensive alliance, or face the consequences."

Hideo's fingers twitched involuntarily. Images of WWII and the brutal acts committed by his forebears filled his mind. "We are not the same nation as we were then," he protested, "and neither are you. But we also will not interfere with China's pursuits."

President Zheng leaned in, his expression cold and unreadable. "Prime Minister, do you know how many Chinese souls were taken by your country during the war?"

The question hung in the air. Hideo felt as though a vice was tightening around his chest. "Four million," he whispered.

"Indeed. Four million," Zheng responded, his voice dripping with bitterness. "You refuse our alliance, and yet you expect us to forget the past. I can snap my fingers and erase one of your largest cities, along with one million of your citizens. Perhaps a mere quarter of our loss, but a taste of what's to come if Japan doesn't realign its stance."

"But China accepted our unconditional surrender in Nanjing! We accepted all of the terms so both sides could move past that terrible era."

"You are confused, Prime Minister. Your surrender was accepted by a dead regime corrupted by Western capitalism. The People never accepted your surrender."

Prime Minister Hideo remembered the nuance often forgotten in his history books. The Republic of China had accepted Japan's surrender in 1945, but in 1949, the Chinese Communist Party overthrew the government and created the People's Republic of China.

Hideo's voice trembled, betraying the torrent of emotions beneath. "You can't mean that. This is a new era, President Zheng. Our nations should be building bridges, not revisiting old wounds."

Zheng's eyes darkened. "It's you who chooses to open old wounds by refusing our hand of alliance. Every action has its price."

With a sudden, chilling clarity, Hideo understood. The ultimatum was more than a mere power play; it was vengeful retribution. The sins of the past still haunted the present.

Struggling to control his rising panic, Hideo tried one last desperate plea. "There must be another way, a compromise. We can negotiate terms, come to an understanding. Don't sacrifice innocent lives for the mistakes of Imperial Japan."

Zheng's gaze didn't waver. "The time for negotiations has passed, Prime Minister. Your decision seals Japan's fate."

And with that final, chilling statement, the screen went black. The silence in the room was stifling. Hideo slumped in his chair. His advisers exchanged fearful glances, none daring to voice the thoughts they all shared. A shadow had fallen over Japan, casting a pall of uncertainty and dread.

9

Near Shikoku Island

At the strike of midnight, the torpedo became active, its computer coming to life with a flurry of electrical activity. It fine-tuned its orientation and silently approached the surface, with internal reaction wheels rotating just enough to orient its glass cone and antenna to peek out of the surface. A signal, encrypted and tightly focused, streamed to the torpedo from satellites above. The torpedo's onboard systems decrypted the message which included target coordinates and a launch time. The torpedo's neural chip quickly calculated a firing solution with an update from the celestial navigation system.

After confirming the message's authenticity, the torpedo descended back into the depths. It floated in the darkness, nose pointed upward, like a snake waiting to strike at an unsuspecting prey. Its inertial navigation systems continued to work and allowed the neural engine to update its firing solution in real time, even as ocean currents ebbed and flowed.

Time seemed to stand still in the darkness of the Pacific, but the torpedo was a cauldron of activity. Its internal systems, running checks and simulations, determined the exact propulsion needed to break the water's surface at the desired velocity. At precisely 3 AM, a distinct mechanical noise resonated from the torpedo. Its hybrid rocket, supplied with onboard oxidizer, began its ignition sequence. A slow, deliberate burn began, controlling the ascent to the surface.

With increasing power and impeccable precision, the torpedo shot upwards, leaving a trail of bubbles in its wake. The water around it churned violently. Faster and faster, the torpedo moved, and as it breached the surface, it was already traveling at 300 kilometers per hour. Above the water, it quickly throttled up and adjusted its angle, moving into Phase 2 of its acceleration. It transformed into a hypersonic water-launched missile!

The night sky greeted the missile as it settled into its flight path. Gravitational forces mounted as it aggressively adjusted to a horizontal angle and deployed delta-shaped wings, flying just 30 meters above the ocean. Within 5 seconds, it reached Mach 3 and could cover over over 60 kilometers per minute.

The ocean blurred beneath. The drone's advanced algorithms took over as it soared north towards Osaka Bay. Coated in a special heat-resistant and radar absorbing polymer, the drone was practically invisible to infrared and radar detection systems.

Sea Dragon's water-launched missile.

10

JS Yari (Japanese Aircraft Carrier)
150 kilometers southeast of Osaka

10 seconds after launch

"Sir, we've detected a submerged rocket launch southwest of Osaka," shouted Sonar Technician Suzuki. "It's likely a submarine-launched missile, unsure of missile type, launched near Shikoku Island."

Captain Tanaka was caught off guard. His surprise quickly morphed into focused determination as he processed the seriousness of the situation. "Suzuki, can you see the missile on radar? I want to know where that missile is headed," he ordered, his voice a controlled calm that belied the adrenaline surging through him.

Suzuki nodded, his fingers dancing over the console, focusing their radar around the launch origin of the missile. Suzuki also pulled in data from their airborne early warning and control (AWACS) system to try and get a better lock on the missile.

30 seconds after launch

"It's small, sir. The stealth of the missile makes it hard to track it definitively even with AWACS, but it looks like it's heading northeast and staying low. This missile is traveling at approximately Mach 3."

Captain Tanaka's mind raced. The potential targets were densely populated areas, likely any of the coastal cities. Osaka? Kyoto? His brother lived in Kyoto… He quickly did the math—at Mach 3, the missile could reach millions of people in less than… 5 minutes. Without hesitation, he grabbed the intercom. "All hands, this is Captain Tanaka. We have a potential threat inbound. Coordinate with the fleet and prepare for countermeasures. I want anti-missile defenses on standby and all aircraft ready for immediate launch. This is not a drill."

As the crew sprang into action, Captain Tanaka turned to his communications officer. "Send the missile's estimated path to all ships in the area and to land-based anti-air defenses. We need a coordinated response."

The communications officer worked quickly, relaying the critical information to the Japanese Self-Defense Forces and allied ships operating nearby. A network of naval and land-based assets began focusing their attention to the approximated path of the missile. Even Japan's advanced radar systems could not get a definitive lock on the missile, but its faint radar reflection was enough to give them a general direction. Could they intercept the missile in time?

60 seconds after launch

"Fire off 10 anti-air missiles in the direction of that weapon, anticipating its course," barked Tanaka. "We need to stop it as soon as possible!"

"Yes sir," Combat Systems Officer Yoshihara responded, "We are unable to confirm a lock on the missile due to its stealth. The firing solution is incomplete."

"Estimate the firing solution and set them to active homing. These missiles need to seek and lock on their own when they're closer to the target."

"Yes sir, launching now."

10 anti-air missiles fired off in quick succession from the *Yari*, barreling towards the missile's projected flight path at Mach 5. Because the radar cross section of the enemy missile was so small, the *Yari* was unable to provide a lock. Each anti-air missile would need to rely on its own onboard radar system to find the target.

90 seconds after launch

Sea Dragon's missile barreled north, following a flight path above the water of Wakayama Bay. Its onboard radar warning receiver (RWR) detected incoming signals from the southeast. At Mach 3, the drone knew it could still be intercepted by anti-air defenses. It quickly adjusted its flight path to fly perpendicular to the direction of the radar pings to minimize its radar signal, and it dropped altitude to just a few meters above the water. It flew like this for about 10 seconds before adjusting its direction back towards Osaka. It angled upwards and released radar-reflecting chaff. Several of the anti-air missiles plunged into the water as they attempted to anticipate the course of the target, and the remaining anti-air missiles quickly lost sight of the drone and locked on to chaff. Because the drone remained at low altitude, it was difficult for other radar systems to detect it from afar.

120 seconds after launch

Once the missile reached the edge of Osaka Bay, it adjusted its angle of flight upwards and began climbing. Its radar systems detected fighter jets scrambling below, but none of Japan's jets or air-to-air defenses could definitively get a lock on it. As atmosphere thinned, it was able to accelerate up to Mach 5. It reached an altitude of 4000 meters in less than five seconds and leveled out.

Onboard RWR raised alarms constantly. Every air defense system was trying to target it, and at Mach 5 its heat signature would soon be detected by infrared sensors. But that wouldn't matter for long.

150 seconds after launch

The missile's computer confirmed its coordinates above the geographic center of Osaka, at an altitude of 4000 meters.

11

4000 meters above Osaka

Nanosecond 1: Inside the spherical warhead is a smaller metal sphere containing Plutonium-239 and Deuterium-tritium gas. The nuclear sphere, also known as the "pit," is wrapped in an explosive compound. An explosive charge detonates, compressing this pit to more than several million atmospheres. This compression reduces the Plutonium-239 to a third of its original size while an adjacent neutron generator fires a shower of neutrons toward the pit. These neutrons collide with the Plutonium-239, and any that miss are reflected by a Beryllium backstop. This intense neutron bombardment triggers a chain reaction of nuclear fission, where Plutonium-239 nuclei split into smaller fragments, releasing nuclear energy and more neutrons.

Nanoseconds 2-10: The core rapidly undergoes fission, releasing a tremendous amount of heat and radiation. The core temperature skyrockets as atoms split, emitting gamma rays, beta particles, and more neutrons. The temperature spikes to over 100 million degrees

Kelvin, hotter than the sun. These high-speed neutrons produce additional fission reactions and initiate fusion in the Deuterium-tritium gas around the core, forming helium and more neutrons. The fusion energy and additional neutrons trigger an unstoppable cascade of nuclear reactions.

Nanoseconds 11-20: The fusion and fission reactions release a huge amount of energy, which hits a second compartment of the warhead containing a Uranium-235 core wrapped around Lithium deuteride. Neutrons collide with the Uranium to form unstable Uranium-236, which splits into Barium and Krypton, releasing a burst of energy and 2-3 additional neutrons per reaction. The intense radiation creates massive pressure, forcing the atoms to overcome their natural electrostatic repulsion, allowing the positively charged nuclei to get close enough for the strong nuclear force to bind them together. Neutrons collide with Lithium-6, breaking it into one tritium and one helium atom.

Nanoseconds 21-50: X-rays and gamma rays transfer energy to the surrounding layers of the bomb, causing them to rapidly heat up and expand. As the fusion reactions continue, the pressure and temperature in the core increase further, driving additional fusion and making the bomb more unstable. Tritium formed by the fission of Lithium-6 fuses with deuterium, releasing helium and additional neutrons.

Nanoseconds 51-100: The intense energy released by both the fission and fusion reactions causes the bomb's core to expand at an incredible rate. The combination of pressure, heat, and radiation pushes against the surrounding layers of the bomb, compressing and heating them to extreme temperatures. The resulting shockwave travels outward, compressing the bomb's casing and initiating further fusion reactions in the surrounding layers.

Nanoseconds 101-200: The pressure and temperature in the core reach a critical threshold where the entire bomb is on the verge of disintegration. The bomb's casing can no longer contain the explosive forces within. At this point, the bomb's materials experience a violent, catastrophic failure. The casing ruptures, releasing an unimaginable amount of energy in a blinding flash of light. The shockwave expands outward at supersonic speeds, accompanied by a deafening roar, annihilating everything in its path.

The released energy continues to expand, creating a huge mushroom cloud. The intense heat, radiation, and shockwave cause widespread devastation in the surrounding area. The explosion's aftermath includes fallout, with radioactive particles carried by wind and atmosphere, spreading the destructive impact far beyond the immediate blast zone.

In a matter of seconds, a fireball three kilometers wide envelops the region and vaporizes everything within. Nearly everyone within an eight kilometer radius of the blast center dies immediately. Osaka absorbs a two-megaton nuclear explosion. A mushroom cloud more than 15 kilometers high forms, spraying radioactive dust and debris around. The cloud is five times taller than Mt. Fuji.

The nuclear attack on Osaka, Japan.

12

The horizon was painted with anguish. Red and orange plumes clouded the sky, smoke rising from the ashen remnants of what once were bustling cities. The devastation was unprecedented. Osaka was now a wasteland of destruction.

The deafening silence that followed the detonation was more haunting than the explosion itself. Streets that once echoed with life now only whispered with the sighs of the wind. One million souls vanished immediately, with another 800,000 expected to die from their wounds over the next week. An entire chapter of history was erased in mere moments. Over three million people were injured.

Amidst the chaos, Prime Minister Hideo Suzuki's phone buzzed to life. His hands trembling, face drained of color, he quickly dialed a number. He was connected almost instantly.

"Zheng!" Hideo's voice cracked, desperation evident in every word. "What have you done?"

The voice on the other end was cold, calculated. "A lesson, Prime Minister. China never forgets."

Tears streamed down Hideo's face as he choked back his emotions. "Our people... they had nothing to do with our past! You're a monster!"

A heavy silence hung between the two leaders.

"I beg you," Hideo continued, voice barely above a whisper. "Please, stop. We'll join the alliance, just... No more!"

There was a pause on the line, before Zheng's voice cut through, dripping with satisfaction. "Congratulations, Prime Minister, on making a wise decision. Welcome to the alliance. Consider the war debt repaid."

Hideo's chest tightened. "Life for life?" he murmured, grappling with the enormity of the compromise he'd just made.

"Exactly," Zheng replied. "Life for life. Your forefathers took from us, and now balance has been restored. But with you now aligned with us, we can look to the future. A future where the Pacific is safe, stable, and prosperous."

Hideo took a shaky breath. "Nothing can be worth the price we have paid."

Zheng's tone softened, if only slightly. "Time will tell, Prime Minister. Together, our grip on the Pacific is unbreakable. We're a force to be reckoned with, an alliance that will rival any other. You may feel the pain now, but generations from now your descendants will look back at this moment as the birth of the New Order in Asia."

The call ended, leaving Hideo staring out at the burning horizon. A mushroom cloud taller than Mount Fuji reminded him of his failure as a leader. Japan would be safe from further aggression, but the price was dear.

In Beijing, President Zheng leaned back in his chair, a look of triumph in his eyes. On his wall, the map of the Asia Pacific region now showed GEATO covering most of East and Southeast Asia. With Japan's inclusion, China's sphere of influence was now unparalleled, giving it dominance over one of the world's most strategically important regions.

Whispers and murmurs spread throughout international circles. China's move was bold, and the consequences of its actions would shape global politics for generations to come. The defensive alliance, now stretching from the northern islands of Japan to the southern reaches of Indonesia, was a titan of power.

China's ascent had been meteoric. Its technological advancements, coupled with strategic alliances, had positioned it as a global superpower. With the Pacific under its control, it had naval and trade routes that would be the envy of nations.

NATO, which once stood as an unchallenged pillar of Western power, now found itself looking across the world at a formidable foe. The balance of power had shifted, and the world had entered a new era of geopolitics.

Japan's integration into the alliance was met with a mixture of anger, relief, and trepidation by its citizens. While the immediate threat had been neutralized, the trauma of the attack and the memory of the lives lost would forever be etched into the national psyche.

Across cities and villages, memorial services were held, and people mourned. They mourned for the lives lost, for the innocence stolen, and for a world that seemed to have gone mad. Amidst the sorrow, however, was a glimmer of hope. Hope that, with the forging of this new alliance, peace could finally prevail.

The Asia Pacific was the heartbeat of a new global order. And at its helm was China, its gaze firmly set on the future.

Part Four

Quantum Chaos

1

The White House

In the dimly lit situation room, President Phelps clenched his briefing papers. He looked down at the report in front of him.

```
FM    AIR FORCE TECHNICAL APPLICATIONS CENTER
TO    SECRETARY OF DEFENSE
SUBJ  CHINESE NUCLEAR ATTACK ON JAPAN
TOP SECRET
1. ONE NUCLEAR EXPLOSION DETECTED OVER OSAKA, JAPAN
2. WATER-LAUNCHED HYPERSONIC WEAPON, STEALTH
3. 2 MEGATON AIRBURST AT 13,000 FEET
4. ESTIMATED 1.5M - 2M FATALITIES, 3M - 4M INJURIES
```

"What do you mean China nuked Japan?" he demanded, his eyes fixed on Secretary of Defense Mark Waid. The room was thick with tension.

"Sir," Waid began. "It seems China's been quietly preparing for this moment for years. Japan's neutral stance kept the country out of China's crosshairs for a while, but China has accumulated so much military strength that it no longer cares for neutrality. They've sent the world a message: You're with us or you're against us."

"But this is insanity!" Phelps exclaimed. "Launching a nuke isn't a mere show of force—it's all out war! How did things spiral out of control like this?"

Before Waid could respond, the red phone at the center of the table rang, its shrill tone slicing through the heavy silence. It was Director Lin.

"Mr. President," Lin's voice came through, sharp and clear, "The CIA has received some intelligence from the Navy that might help."

Phelps leaned in, "Talk to me, Lin."

"Our naval patrols around the Japanese waters detected an anomaly. Just before the nuke hit, one of our submarines caught an unfamiliar underwater sound signature—like a rocket being fired at hypersonic speeds. It's our belief that this missile came from the depths, from a newly developed submarine. Our submarine didn't hear the enemy submarine or even detect it after the launch."

Phelps' forehead creased, "We didn't find the submarine? I thought a missile launch gives away the position of a submarine immediately."

Lin sighed, "That's why this is different, sir. We heard the missile, but the sub was nowhere near the launch site. We've been tracking China's advancements in stealth tech, and one of our field agents recently uncovered some intel on the China coast. China released a new type of submarine from a concealed dock. It's undetectable to conventional systems. Given its design, and the fact it hasn't docked or even attempted to surface anywhere since we learned about it… We think it's unmanned."

"An unmanned, nuclear-armed submarine?" asked Phelps.

"Yes. It would be far ahead of anything we have in our portfolio. No supercomputer we have can stay cool enough to pilot a large submarine in realtime. The sensor inputs and controls, strategic decision-making, and communications are too much for modern AI to process simultaneously. Our experts still can't believe the Chinese were able to surpass our AI capabilities."

"But we invented AI!" Phelps pounded the table. "A stealth submarine with AI, more advanced than our own, and the power to launch nuclear missiles at any coastal city without detection? We're looking at a weapon that could tilt global power dynamics. How did they get this far without us knowing about it?"

"We can debrief you on that later, Mr. President," said Lin. "I think we should focus on addressing the threat and containing this right now."

Waid interjected. "Mr. President, given Japan's isolation, our usual routes of intervention are blocked. Diplomatically, if we act in Japan's defense, it would only escalate matters. Militarily, a direct confrontation with China risks nuclear escalation. However, a surgical strike on the submarine might just give us a chance to reset the playing field."

Lin added, "With the right resources and coordination between the CIA and the DoD, we might be able to hack into the sub's communication system. But we'd need to get close—very close."

Phelps took a deep breath. "Do it. I want the CIA and military to collaborate on this. If we can neutralize this submarine without triggering a full-scale war, we must. And we need to strike fear into the Chinese so they don't push their defensive alliance any further. It's bad enough already if they've got Japan to sign on to it. Even if they were coerced."

Waid nodded, "We'll need to deploy a specialist team with the Navy's backing. They can approach the submarine discreetly and attempt an intervention."

Lin agreed, "The CIA has cyber experts who've been training for scenarios just like this. With the Navy's firepower and our expertise, I think we can succeed."

Phelps' face hardened with resolve. "Then let's move. Time is of the essence. While we can't defend Japan in the traditional sense, we can ensure that China doesn't wield unchecked power with this weapon. Assemble your teams. I want updates every hour."

2

President Phelps tapped his fingers on the desk of the Oval Office, waiting for a post-quantum encrypted connection to be established. Diplomatic ties with China had soured over the last decade, and he was uncertain if Beijing would even answer.

The line clicked, and a composed voice came through. "President Phelps, to what do I owe this unexpected call?" said Zheng Song Han.

Phelps took a deep breath. "President Zheng, the attack on Japan crossed a line. What were you thinking?"

Zheng's tone remained calm but carried an edge. "We needed to send a clear message to Asia. Japan's historical transgressions have not been forgotten."

Phelps' grip tightened on the receiver. "We practically handed you Taiwan to avoid conflict. The agreement was clear: Let you retake the island unchallenged, and in return, you play nicely with the West and be a good trading partner. Why ruin that arrangement?"

Zheng's voice grew sharper. "Do you recall your history, Phelps? The West has deceived China countless times. Opium wars, Hong Kong's seizure, the betrayal at

Tsingtao—our history is riddled with Western exploitation. We will not be subjugated again."

Phelps leaned forward, his voice stern. "That was another era. The world has moved on to focus on domestic issues. The US isn't interested in manipulating Asian politics anymore."

Zheng scoffed. "Please. The US is constantly trying to undermine the CCP with its perverted ideologies. Hollywood is your mouthpiece, polluting the world with perverted ideas that we do not care for. Your corporations pollute our people with selfish consumerism. And your Ivy League poisons the minds of our students with the wildest and most ludicrous ideas I've ever heard of. We're done with the West."

"So this is your strategy now? Total conquest of Asia and isolationism? Are you ready to face the consequences?"

"You misunderstand, President Phelps," Zheng replied smoothly. "We are consolidating our power within Asia to prevent further incursions. Japan's integration into our sphere is crucial. We seek coexistence, not conflict."

Phelps was incredulous. "Coexistence through intimidation and force? This path you're on is dangerous. You of all people should know that forceful seizure of alliances never ends well."

Zheng chuckled, a low, menacing sound. "You talk of danger when your military bases encircle us, when you arm our adversaries. Your nuclear submarines once docked 500 miles away in the Philippines. We are putting an end to easy Western access to the Asia Pacific. We will guide the region forward—without your influence."

"History tells us that imperialism never ends well. You're repeating the mistakes of the past thousand years."

"That's a funny statement to hear from the President of the United States. Your country wrote the book on imperialism. We studied your failures and will not repeat your mistakes, just as we learned how to leverage capitalism without allowing the disease of democracy to poison our people."

Phelps steadied his nerves. "This isn't the future we should be building, Zheng. We have an opportunity to collaborate, not through coercion, but through diplomacy and cooperation."

"China has been disrespected and underestimated for too long. That ends now."

"If you continue down this path, the US will have to respond. Don't do this!"

"Then we will be prepared. Stay out of our affairs, and we'll stay out of yours. But if you interfere, there will be consequences. This is an Asian matter. No matter your actions, we are ready for what comes next. Are you?"

Phelps' silence was the only answer he could muster. The line went dead. He stared at the receiver, his mind racing.

3

Evolve Martial Arts Academy - McLean, Virginia

Grace never liked exercising at the CIA campus gym—it was too plain for her. But the mixed martial arts gym a few miles away was more to her liking. It had just the right mix of blood and sweat. Grace stood before the heavy bag, her fists wrapped, her mind ablaze with a tumult of emotions. She heard the news that morning. The destruction of Osaka was a preview of what could happen to other parts of Asia. Would the CCP go after South Korea next? She unleashed a flurry of punches and kicks while contemplating the CCP's next move.

Grace tried to steady her breathing, to focus on the form and discipline that Muay Thai demanded. Yet, with each strike, images of the devastation in Osaka flashed before her eyes—buildings reduced to rubble, streets once vibrant with life now silent, and the countless faces of those who had perished. Her heart ached for the victims and their families, and a fierce anger took root within her, fueling her strikes with a power she seldom felt.

The gym around her blurred into the background, the sounds of other students drowned out by the pain she felt with every punch. Grace was alone in her battle, facing an unseen enemy with every fiber of her being. The heavy bag before her transformed into a stand-in for those who had dared to inflict such pain on innocent lives.

Each strike was delivered with precision, honed by years of training, but now imbued with a raw, unfiltered passion. Sweat beaded on her brow, tracing paths down her face and neck, the physical exertion an echo of the storm raging within her.

This was no longer just about duty; it was personal. The attack on Osaka had crossed a line, and she felt a deep, visceral need to respond, to take action, to make those responsible pay for their crimes. She punched the bag harder.

Yet, beneath the surface of her anger and resolve, Grace wrestled with a sense of helplessness. She was one person in a vast, intricate game of international politics and warfare. The enormity of the situation, the complexity of the geopolitical landscape, threatened to overwhelm her. What could she do?

But as she stood there, drenched in sweat, breathing heavily, she realized that this was precisely why she had joined the CIA. Not because she believed she could single-handedly change the world, but because she refused to stand by and do nothing. In the face of injustice, she would fight, with every tool at her disposal, every skill she had honed. Grace Kim was not just an agent; she was a warrior.

Her gaze hardened, and she took a step back from the heavy bag, observing the marks of her fury, the physical evidence of her inner turmoil. She knew the road ahead would be fraught with danger and uncertainty. Yet, the fire within her burned hotter than ever. She would channel her anger, her pain, and her longing for justice into her mission. For Osaka and for the countless others who suffered at the hands of tyrants and aggressors, she would fight. And she would not rest until she had done everything within her power to make right what had been so grievously wronged. She would make the CCP pay for their war crimes.

Grace wiped the sweat from her brow, her eyes reflecting a resolve as unyielding as steel. She was ready. Ready to face whatever lay ahead, ready to bear the weight of her duty, and ready to strike back against the darkness that sought to engulf the world.

4

Langley, Virginia

"If we can spoof the sound signature of a known Chinese battleship, we might be able to make this work," Marvin said to Grace as they looked over a dozen scattered pages of his plan—which amounted to little more than scribblings and equations at this point.

"What do you mean?" Asked Grace.

"Well, imagine you're this super stealthy submarine. You don't want to give away your position by broadcasting any communications, even if it is to identify another ship. Maybe the submarine receives radio signals instructing it to surface, but most of the time it likely uses sound signatures to identify hostile and allied ships."

"You're basing this off of a hunch?"

"I used to read a lot of submarine novels as a kid. Plus, I talked to some of the intelligence folks at the Navy and they told me our submarines do the same thing. Each submarine carries a database of engine sound signatures —it can tell what's a frigate, what's a battleship, and so on. Assuming the submarine has a list of all its ships in service, it can even identify ships by name."

"Okay, so if we can somehow spoof a Chinese ship audio signature, we can sail right up to the submarine and then hack it?"

"Not quite. The submarine likely has an authentication process to validate the identity of the other ship. Even if we knew the Chinese encryption protocol for their communications, we don't have the digital certificate needed to validate our identity to the submarine."

"And so how do we get a certificate?" Grace looked intrigued.

"That's the hardest part. Not only do we need to get a signed digital certificate from Beijing's Naval command, but also we'd need to make sure our ship is on the Submarine's manifest of trusted ships. The submarine won't trust a ship that doesn't exist on the approved list, even with a valid digital certificate from PLA headquarters."

"Could we break into Beijing's Naval HQ and patch you in to their network to get all this stuff done?"

"Even if I were sitting in front of Beijing's central computer, it would take me days to hack that system. And the certificate signing requests are only approved on a case by case basis by military leadership. We might be able to force someone to approve the certificate signing request at gunpoint, but that's really risky. And the submarine probably doesn't update its manifest list of trusted ships except at special scheduled times. Honestly, it would be easier for us to hijack a ship and exploit their radio system to talk to the submarine."

"What if we did that? We could steal a Chinese destroyer so we can use its sound signature to talk to a stealth AI-powered submarine. That can't be hard, can it?" Grace muttered sarcastically.

"Maybe there's a simpler way that we're not seeing. Let me think on this and get back to you tomorrow."

5

The early morning light crept lazily through the curtains of Marvin's hotel room, a stark contrast to the frenetic energy that had consumed the past several days. He and Grace had been in a whirlwind of planning, strategizing every possible angle of their upcoming mission. It was a plan forged in urgency and necessity, not perfect, but their best shot given the constraints of time.

Today, however, was a brief respite—a day of mandated rest and recovery before they plunged into the unknown. Marvin's mind was still tangled in the details of their scheme when his phone's ringtone sliced through his thoughts. It was Grace, punctual as ever.

"Hey Marvin, free for some exercise?" she asked, her voice crisp and alert. "Let's go for a run. It might be the last fresh air we get for a while if we're deploying tomorrow."

Marvin, still groggy from sleep, agreed and suggested the CIA running track. But Grace was quick to dismiss that idea. "No, we can't talk around Langley; too many prying ears, and the whole place is covered in microphones. I'll pick you up. Come out to the parking lot in 15 minutes."

Still groggy from lack of sleep, Marvin slipped on his running shoes. He made his way to the parking lot, where Grace was waiting in a nondescript grey sedan.

The drive to Washington DC was quiet, each lost in their own thoughts. Marvin gazed out the window, noting the familiar landmarks as they passed. He hadn't realized how close CIA headquarters was to the National Mall. He last visited the Mall on a field trip in elementary school. The innocent wonder of that visit felt like a lifetime away, now replaced by the weight of his responsibilities as a CIA operative. As they parked near the Mall, Marvin couldn't help but reflect on the strange twist of fate that had brought him back to this place.

They stepped out of the car and began to run. They headed to the Washington Monument and finished a few laps. The early morning breeze was refreshing, a gentle reprieve from the tension that had built up over the past days. As they jogged, the city slowly woke around them, oblivious to the drama unfolding overseas.

Marvin and Grace found a secluded bench near a row of cherry trees nearby, their leaves painting the sky with orange and brown on this cold autumn day. In 2024, Japan had donated these cherry trees to the United States to commemorate the upcoming 250th anniversary of the Declaration of Independence. The US and Japan were the closest of allies at that time. Nobody could have predicted the intensity of nationalist fervor that swept Japan in the decades that followed. Japan adopted an isolationist stance and expelled the US military from its shores. But the cherry trees stood, a reminder of the alliance the two countries once enjoyed.

"Grace, can I ask you something?" Marvin sat down, looking at Grace as she used the bench to stretch her legs.

"Sure, what's up?" Grace replied, her gaze meeting his with an open curiosity.

Marvin hesitated for a moment before delving into his question. "I don't know much about you besides what you told me on our fake dates, and I don't even know if any of that was true. I was just curious about where you're really from. Why did you join the CIA?"

Grace smiled faintly, a mix of amusement in her eyes. "Most of what I told you was actually true, Marvin. Except, well, I obviously wasn't a medical student at UCSF. I studied Political Science at UC Berkeley. The day China imposed the blockade on Taiwan is the day I decided to join the CIA. I was worried China would go after Korea next."

Marvin listened intently, trying to understand Grace's personal interest in their mission. "You're super smart, talented—you could probably have succeeded at any job. So why make below average pay to put your life on the line, miss holidays with your family, and travel all the time? This kind of life can't be easy."

Grace laughed, a sound that seemed to embody both the challenge and the thrill of their chosen path. "It definitely isn't. But I'm young and I want to make a difference. I'll think about settling down and living a normal life one day… Just not any time soon. I joined for a lot of the same reasons you joined, Marvin. The desire to do something real. We're the tip of the spear. When you hear a news headline about some military coup in some no-name country, chances are we had something to do with it. We're literally shaping the future in the shadows. I wanted to fight back. I knew that after Taiwan, South Korea might be next. I still have family in South Korea."

"Does the CIA really overthrow dictators and do all that cloak-and-dagger stuff?"

Grace laughed. "I can't confirm or deny."

Marvin continued. "I mostly joined the CIA because I want to help protect us from threats… I guess you could say I believe in the right of self-defense. I've never thought about being used in an offensive manner. I feel a bit torn about our mission because we're leaving the realm of self-defense, and instead intervening in foreign issues."

Grace's thought for a moment. "Yes, our weaponry and nuclear arsenal protect us from anything the CCP wants to do to us. The CCP hasn't attacked us directly. But would you rather the fight your enemy in your backyard or thousands of miles away in the Pacific? We're pro-actively going out there and driving a knife into the heart of the CCP's plans because we know what happens if they win. They inch closer and closer to our shores until one day they're here. And they're already here."

"What do you mean 'they're already here?'" asked Marvin.

"We tried to play nice with them in the 2010s, and look what happened. The CCP enrolled spies into our universities and installed puppets into our corporations. They used social media to manipulate our beliefs and spy on our people. I could tell you all the headline reasons like 'the CCP's threat to democracy' or 'human rights violations' but the real reason we're acting is that we don't like seeing a power imbalance that could threaten our interests. And the CCP is getting too strong to be ignored now. We have to stop them before they get even stronger."

Marvin absorbed her words, a new understanding dawning in his eyes. "I never thought about it that way. So we proactively try to shape the world?"

"Yes, that's why the US does everything. Every dollar spent, every policy decision made is to either insulate us from threats or allow us to shape the world into an ally. Do you think we give food aid to developing countries out of the goodness of our hearts? Marvin, it's all for influence. And UN grain shipments are amazing covers for our operatives to deploy into any country. If you want to find a way to overthrow a regime in some war torn country, just attach a few field operatives to an NGO that delivers vaccines or clean drinking water. Once we're in, we get to work. It's our best cover."

Marvin's expression was a mix of realization and concern.

Grace's gaze softened, reassuring yet serious. "Don't worry, as long as the people in charge are using us for the right reasons, everything we do is in the national interest. And don't get me wrong, I'm not a zealot—I know that America isn't perfect and never will be. But the world needs something to shape it, and I'd rather it be an imperfect republic than a perfect dictatorship."

A brief silence fell between them. Marvin finally broke the stillness. "Are you nervous about our mission?"

Grace's eyes held a determined glint as she responded. "I'm not going to sugarcoat it. It's going to be hard. And for your first deployment, it's a lot of pressure. But if we fail, the CCP wins. And if that happens, Asia is doomed."

Grace paused. "How do you feel about going up against China?" she added. "Any hesitations?"

Marvin's expression was resolute, his voice tinged with a mix of conviction and personal conflict. "Don't get me wrong, I've got no loyalties to the CCP. Sure, my family is Chinese, but the CCP doesn't speak for us all. For China to thrive and coexist with the world peacefully, I think the CCP needs to end."

The conversation paused as they both took a moment to reflect. It was a moment that underscored the nuanced nature of their roles—personal histories and national duties intertwined in an intricate dance.

Grace broke the silence, her tone shifting to one of camaraderie and reassurance. "Look, Marvin, we're in this together. Our backgrounds, our reasons for being here, they might be different, but our goal is the same. We protect our country, and sometimes that means making difficult choices. But remember, you're not alone in this. We're a team."

Marvin nodded. "Thanks, Grace. It means a lot to hear that. It's just a lot to comprehend. The real impact of what we do, the lives that are affected. Six months ago I was working a 9-to-5 job testing firewalls for a cybersecurity company. Now I'm about to board a submarine and stop nuclear war."

Grace stood up, stretching her legs, her gaze fixed on the horizon. "It is a lot of pressure. But we'll do great!" She flashed a thumbs-up, smiled, and started running again. She might have been a deadly field operative, but she still had a cute and playful side to her.

The conversation shifted to lighter topics as they made their way back through the quiet streets of Washington DC. The morning was slowly giving way to the hustle and bustle of the day, and with it came a return to their roles as CIA operatives.

6

The next day, Marvin and Grace headed to Langley Air Force Base. When they arrived at the entrance, they showed their badges and asked for the Squadron Commander.

An electric humvee rolled up to the entrance, and out stepped Commander Nichols. "I don't like this one goddamn bit," Nichols said, spitting on the ground. "But you two are coming with me."

They hopped into the humvee. Grace sat in the front and Marvin in the back, and Nichols sat in the driver's seat. Nichols let go of the steering wheel as the self-driving capability took over.

"Look you two, I don't know who you know in the White House but they told me you get everything you need and not to ask too many questions. So, tell me what you need from me."

"Commander Nichols, it's great to meet you. We need the fastest transport possible to these coordinates," Grace said as she handed Nichols a scrap of paper with some coordinates. "There's a time and date on that paper too.

A minute too early or a minute too late and we might not make it."

Nichols punched the numbers into his humvee's map application. "This is in the middle of nowhere in the Pacific Ocean!"

"Exactly. We're linking up with a submarine. They know we're coming. We just need to drop at the surface, and we'll be able to climb aboard."

"A water drop is no problem," Nichols said. "But I do have a problem with the timetable. According to this, we need to fly you about 4800 miles in about 2 hours. Need I remind you that we're on the East Coast?"

"C'mon Commander, you and I both know you have the technology," Grace smiled. "Let's make it happen. President's orders, after all."

Commander Nichols typed a few numbers into his humvee computer screen and connected with the base. "Crew Chief, this is Commander Nichols. Please be advised we have an emergency takeoff request. Two passengers, on the SR-73 Starkiller. Water drop and autonomous takeoff and landing. Make it happen in less than 30 minutes."

"Yes sir, good thing we've got one fueled already," replied the Crew Chief. "Send me the coordinates and I'll plot a course."

Commander Nichols turned to Grace and Marvin. "Look, we haven't tested this very much. So I'm not going to tell you this is 100% safe. But we have two escape pods in the Starkiller which can be dropped out the bomb bay doors. The Starkiller will get you to your coordinates in about an hour. Everything on the ship will be done autonomously, so you need to make sure you are in those escape pods before drop time. The escape pods float and have an hour of air supply, so your Navy buddies will have plenty of time to find you."

"Sounds good," Marvin said, exchanging a glance with Grace. "We're ready."

The humvee pulled up to the hangar, where the sleek, black SR-73 Starkiller awaited them. The hum of activity around the plane was charged with urgency as ground crew moved with precision, ensuring the aircraft was ready for the mission. The SR-73 Starkiller resembled its predecessor, the SR-72 Darkstar. Starkiller, however, was bigger and boasted a significantly greater fuel range. It did sacrifice some velocity (Darkstar could achieve Mach 10 while Starkiller topped out at Mach 8), but it could go deep behind enemy lines to drop nuclear payloads.

"Time to board," Nichols said, leading them to the aircraft. "Remember, the autonomous system will take care of everything. Just be in those pods on time."

Marvin and Grace climbed up the ladder into back of the plane. The interior was sparse but filled with advanced technology. They headed up to the cockpit and strapped themselves into their seats. The peeked out two small windows. Starkiller was mostly piloted by electronics and computers, so the windows were designed for visual guidance rather than for navigation.

"Autonomous system engaged," a robotic voice announced. "Mission parameters received. Launch sequence initiated."

The Starkiller taxied itself to the runway. Its engines roared to life. The onboard computer conducted a systems check. "Combustion is optimal. Sensors online. Initiating aircraft launch in 3…2…1…" Marvin and Grace felt a surge of adrenaline as the plane accelerated down the tarmac and took off into the sky.

The acceleration was intense as the Starkiller broke the sound barrier and continued to climb, gradually increasing altitude and speed until it reached a cruising altitude of 85,000 feet and Mach 8. The world outside the cockpit became a blur as they raced towards their destination.

"Distance to target: 4800 miles. Estimated time of arrival: 55 minutes," the robotic voice updated.

Marvin checked the time and nodded to Grace. "We're on schedule."

Grace looked out the window and admired the view of a big blue earth. At their altitude, they were near the reaches of space.

"You know," Grace said as she turned to Marvin. "If this were any other situation, I'd say this is quite romantic."

"You're kind of weird," Marvin replied. "But for what it's worth I'm glad we're on this mission together. Despite the emotional rollercoaster you put me on by dating me just to recruit me to the CIA, I do enjoy your company."

As the minutes ticked by, the Starkiller maintained its incredible speed, flying autonomously towards the middle of the Pacific Ocean. Grace monitored their progress, her eyes flicking to the timer counting down to their drop.

"Ten minutes to drop," the robotic voice announced.

"Let's get ready," Marvin said. They unstrapped themselves and moved to the escape pods located in the rear of the aircraft. The pods were cramped but equipped with everything they needed for the drop.

"Five minutes to drop. Reducing altitude. Reducing velocity. Initiating pod sequence," the robotic voice continued.

Marvin and Grace secured themselves inside the pods, checked their oxygen supplies and made sure their homing beacons worked.

The Starkiller reduced its altitude to about 3000 feet, and slowed to about 180 mph.

"Drop sequence initiated," the voice said. The bomb bay doors opened, and the pods were released, plummeting towards the ocean below. As they fell, they popped two parachutes and the pods descended towards earth. At 50 feet, explosive bolts on the escape pods disconnected the chute, and the pod quickly fell into the water and floated back to the surface. The Starkiller banked a large turn and headed towards Hawaii for refueling.

A few minutes later, a large submarine surfaced just 100 feet away. A hatch opened, and a surly-looking man with brown hair, stepped out. He held up a bullhorn and shouted, "This is Captain Reese of the USS *Pasadena*. We'll have you aboard in 10 minutes, hang on!"

Reese's crew brought out an inflatable motor raft and went out to each pod. They tapped a wrench on the pod so the inhabitant would know it was time to pop the escape hatch from inside. With a pull of a lever, the roof of the pod popped off and Marvin and Grace climbed out of their respective pods into the raft.

A few moments later, Marvin and Grace climbed up *Pasadena's* conning tower and descended a ladder into the main cabin.

"Close the hatch, bring us down!" barked Captain Reese. The crew carried out his orders and the submarine began its descent.

"Welcome aboard the USS *Pasadena,*" Captain Reese addressed Marvin and Grace. "Now, can one of you tell me why I had to leave my patrol route to pick up two damn CIA operatives?"

Part Five

Quantum Bash

1

USS Pasadena

The team crowded in a dimly lit room, the faint hum of machinery reminding them they were onboard a nuclear submarine with enough firepower to level half of China. Commander Jackson, a veteran Navy SEAL with countless covert operations under his belt, sat with Grace and Marvin at the officer's table. Together, they reviewed the blueprints of the Chinese destroyer, *Tiger Claw.*

"So we're not stealing *Tiger Claw*?" Grace asked.

"No, I came up with something more subtle," Marvin began. "Accessing the *Tiger Claw's* servers is the linchpin. Their central system contains the keystore, which is our golden ticket to the AI submarine. Grace, you'll need to connect the server to a computer I've prepared. It contains a worm designed to wait for the keystore's next use. The worm will grab the keystore and password and send it over to us the next time *Tiger Claw* is near port."

Jackson looked up, his eyes scanning Marvin and Grace. "Sounds solid, but getting her in and out undetected is going to be a hell of a challenge. The *Tiger*

Claw is one of the most advanced destroyers in China's fleet."

Grace smirked, her confidence evident. "Don't worry, commander. Just get me onboard and I'll handle the rest."

Jackson wasn't amused. "Here's how it'll go down: My SEAL team and I will secure a route for insertion. We've identified a weak point—a dive hatch on the port side, underwater. We'll approach in a special submersible to avoid sonar detection. From there, Grace will have to move fast."

Grace pointed to the blueprint. "Here's the central computer hub. It's deep in the belly of the ship, which is both a curse and a blessing. Fewer guards, but it'll take time to get there."

Marvin handed her a slim metallic device. "This is a compact electromagnetic pulse (EMP) generator. It's short-range, but it can unlock electronic doors for you."

"Once I'm in and the worm is deployed, we need an exit strategy," Grace said, concern in her eyes.

Marvin sighed. "The worm installation could take 5 minutes. That leaves you 5 minutes to get to the server room, 5 minutes to install, and maybe 1 minute to get the heck off the boat."

Grace took a deep breath. "Then we better make each second count."

2

One of the first 10 SSN(X) submarines deployed in the 2040s, USS *Pasadena* was one of America's pride, an apex predator of the deep sea. Though built by man, it was almost as elusive as nature's most cunning creatures. The US had maintained undersea superiority for decades, and even China's *Sea Dragon* submarine would likely avoid confrontation with an SSN(X).

Grace and Marvin sat in silence, mentally reviewing details of the upcoming operation. Every person on board understood that they were heading into a difficult mission. Their mission could stop—or start—the next world war.

Captain Reese approached Grace and the SEALs. "We're nearing the coordinates," he whispered, his voice just audible above the muffled sounds of the submarine's inner workings. "You have five minutes."

"Time to move," Grace replied, nodding to the SEAL team.

The team's infiltration submersible sat attached to the *Pasadena's* maintenance hatch. Compact and sleek, the detachable submersible was designed for covert operations. Its exterior was painted in a dark polymer coating to minimize light and sonar reflection, and its fanless water thrusters, powered by the latest in nuclear battery technology, ensured a silent approach.

Grace and the SEAL team took their positions, and submariner Mills from the *Pasadena* took the helm. As they settled in, a soft red light illuminated the submersible's interior. With practiced precision, they initiated the detachment sequence, leaving *Pasadena.* Once detached and clear, *Pasadena* performed a slow turn and headed off towards her next waypoint a few miles away.

Submariner Mills could feel the pulse of the water through the controls. He maneuvered them steadily towards their target using the on-board navigational systems. The fanless thrusters made almost no sound, and the submersible moved like a ghost in the deep.

An hour later, Mills saw the shape of the *Tiger Claw* ahead through their miniature periscope night-vision camera.

"Approaching ship; readying magnetic attachment," Mills whispered, his fingers dancing over the control panel. "Get ready for go-sign."

Drawing closer, they identified the underwater port hatch of the *Tiger Claw.* Mills piloted the submersible just below it, aligning perfectly. With a soft thud, the powerful magnets activated, attaching them securely to the hull of the Chinese destroyer.

Sergeant Laine, an expert in underwater demolitions and breach operations, began preparing the entry equipment. "We've got one shot at this," he murmured, carefully inspecting each tool. The team knew the importance of silence, even more so now that they were physically connected to the enemy. He wired up an explosive strip around the hatch seals. When detonated, it would cut out an outline of the hatch like a cookie cutter through dough. But he had to wait for the right time.

Mills checked the clock. At precisely 12:10 AM, Pasadena would fire two torpedoes towards the *Tiger Claw*. The panic would create enough distraction that the crew would not immediately investigate the small detonation off the side of the ship. They would also need to be fast and get detached from the ship before *Tiger Claw* could accelerate to flank speed. At that speed, the submarine might shear right off the ship.

"Let's do this," Grace whispered, her voice filled with determination. It was time to infiltrate *Tiger Claw*.

3

East China Sea

The crew of *Tiger Claw* was on high alert. The alarm had come suddenly, an unwelcome interruption to the routine of ocean patrol.

"Torpedo doors opening, captain! There is an enemy submarine about 10 kilometers off that is preparing to fire torpedoes!" Sonar Officer Guo reported, his voice laced with urgency. The calm of the bridge was shattered in an instant, replaced by a flurry of activity as the crew sprang into action.

"Man battle stations, evasive maneuvers!" Captain Lee commanded, his voice booming across the bridge. The disbelief in his tone was evident. "How did we miss this submarine?"

As the crew scrambled, Guo shouted, "Torpedoes in the water! I count two, targeting our port side! I recommend evasive maneuvers and countermeasures." They were moments away from impact.

"Flank speed, left full rudder!" Lee ordered, his mind racing through the tactical implications of their next move. By accelerating and turning towards the torpedoes, they could potentially outmaneuver the incoming threat. This bold tactic would momentarily expose their port side to further risk, yet it was a calculated decision in the face of imminent danger.

In the midst of the high-stakes maneuvering, Lee sought more information. "Who fired the torpedoes? Do we have a sound signature?" he pressed, turning to his Sonar Officer for answers.

"Sir, we're picking up a mixture of noisy sound signatures from the torpedo. It's equipped with some kind of stealth masking technology, confounding our passive sonar. It could belong to any country," Guo reported, his analysis adding another layer of complexity to the situation.

Lee pondered the possibilities. "It might be the Japanese," he mused internally. Relations between China and Japan were strained, despite the uneasy alliance. The CCP had not encountered Japan's newer submarines, leaving a gap in their intelligence. Japan's prowess in developing ultra-quiet attack submarines was well-known, and the prospect of a rogue Japanese commander taking advantage of this technological edge to launch an untraceable attack was a concerning possibility.

"Call Beijing and let them know we may have been attacked by an enemy submarine, possibly a Japanese attack submarine," Lee commanded, directing his order to the radio operator. The implication of such an act was grave, signaling a potential escalation in hostilities.

As the crew busied themselves with their assigned tasks, the tension aboard the *Tiger Claw* reached a fever pitch. Alarms continued to blare, tracking the incoming torpedoes as the ship executed its daring evasive action.

The bridge was a hive of activity, each officer and crew member performing their role with a precision honed by rigorous training and the adrenaline of the moment.

As Captain Lee navigated the immediate threat, his mind was already racing ahead, considering the implications of this encounter. The sound masking technology used by the torpedoes was a clear indication that they were dealing with a sophisticated and formidable opponent. The need for vigilance was greater than ever, as the murky waters of international relations seemed to mirror the dark, unforgiving depths of the ocean they sailed.

Amidst the chaos, nobody noticed a small underwater detonation off the ship's port side.

4

Two SEALs prepared to enter the belly of *Tiger Claw.* With loaded rifles, they breached the hatch door, only to find the space deserted. The recent offensive actions from the *Pasadena* had effectively lured the crew of the *Tiger Claw* to their battle stations, leaving this section of the ship eerily quiet. Grace followed closely behind, her senses heightened as she scanned the immediate area for any signs of danger. Finding none, she signaled the all-clear to her companions with a confident thumbs up, prompting their withdrawal back to the infiltration submarine. Now, Grace stood alone, a solitary figure amidst the vastness of the enemy's lair.

Jackson watched as Grace snuck into the depths of *Tiger Claw*. He grabbed a 10-pound EPX-2 explosive charge and programmed the detonator.

"Time until torpedo impact?" Jackson asked submariner Mills.

"I calculate 10 minutes and 39 seconds."

"Great. Prepare the ship for detachment at the 10 minute mark."

Jackson punched 10 minutes into his detonator. Meanwhile, his crew re-sealed the Chinese maintenance hatch and applied a thin strip of Qwik-weld. The special polymer was like super glue, and it would provide temporary protection from leakage for 10 minutes. The hull of the ship would be torn to shreds soon, hiding any evidence of their boarding party. The team worked quickly—they had about 30 seconds to finish the job before *Tiger Claw* accelerated past their safe attachment velocity.

"Qwik-weld applied, shutting hatch!" Jackson exclaimed to Mills. Five seconds left.

"Shutting outer hatch, aye, preparing to detach magnets," Mills whispered.

And with a quick turn, the submarine sealed its inner hatch and detached from the hull of the Tiger Claw and descended to 100 feet, and then quietly drifted away in silence.

5

Grace wore an imitation PLA Navy officer uniform. She possessed a functional knowledge of Mandarin, enough to potentially defuse any casual encounters with the ship's personnel. Fortunately for Grace, the crew was preoccupied with the threat of *Pasadena's* incoming torpedoes.

The ship was in high alert from the torpedo warning. Grace recognized the advantage this chaos presented; the crew's focus on the impending danger allowed her to quicken her pace, her movements becoming more purposeful as she made her way deeper into the heart of the battleship.

The ship's electronic door keypads, designed to thwart unauthorized access, proved no match for the specialized equipment Marvin had given her. She bypassed these defenses with ease, her progress through the ship unimpeded as she approached the central nerve center of *Tiger Claw*—the server room.

Inside, the glow of numerous screens and blinking lights greeted her. Quickly locating an access port, she reached under her uniform and pulled out a small tablet computer. She activated the screen and wired the tablet to the access port. Her fingers flew across the on-screen keyboard, a ballet of precision and speed, as she navigated through layers of security protocols. The progress bar on her screen slowly inched forward.

Grace's concentration was shattered by an unexpected sound—footsteps approaching, accompanied by the murmur of voices. Instantly alert, she realized her vulnerable position; discovery here, in the very heart of the enemy's domain, would be catastrophic. She could not afford to be caught in the ship's server room—punishment would be torture and death.

With no time to spare, Grace made a swift decision. She slipped into the shadows, her heart racing as the voices grew nearer. Her mind raced through potential escape routes and contingencies, knowing that each passing second increased the risk of discovery. She reached under her uniform skirt for a 9mm pistol and aimed it at the doorway. She lined up the tritium sights with the door.

As the voices in the corridor grew louder, indicating the imminent arrival of the ship's crew, Grace prepared herself for what might come next. If she fired rounds here, she would attract even more guards. Suicide was preferable to capture, so she would need to save a bullet for herself.

6

The USS *Pasadena* had fired two torpedoes at *Tiger Claw*. As *Tiger Claw* began evasive maneuvers, *Sea Dragon*, lurking just two kilometers away, detected the launch. Her onboard computer rapidly calculated the bearing and distance to *Pasadena*. Without hesitation, she turned to face her target, calculated a firing solution, and unleashed two Yu-7 torpedoes. To avoid revealing her position with active sonar, *Sea Dragon* programmed her torpedoes to navigate to Pasadena's last known location and initiate their own active search.

Pasadena was abuzz with activity. "Conn, Sonar!" Ensign Clarke's urgent voice pierced the silence. "Two torpedo launches detected, approximately 6.5 nautical miles away bearing 300 degrees, closing fast! Speed is approximately 50 knots. Time to impact: 8.5 minutes."

Captain Reese sprang into action. "Right full rudder, bring us to course 120 degrees. WEPS, open aft torpedo tubes and prepare a firing solution. On my count, fire off two torpedoes.[7] We need to put some distance between us and those incoming torpedoes."

---

[7] "WEPS" refers to the Weapons Officer on a US Submarine.

"Aye aye, Captain," executive officer (XO) Smith echoed, as he and the crew executed the orders with practiced precision.

"Conn, WEPS," the intercom crackled. "Tubes 1 and 2 are open and ready, firing solution locked."

"WEPS, Conn. Fire when ready," Captain Reese commanded.

Pasadena launched two torpedoes and surged to flank speed. At 40 knots, they couldn't outrun the enemy torpedoes but could buy precious time.

"Find me a place to hide," Reese demanded. "Is there anything on the map?"

"Sir," replied Smith, "Our topographical system shows an underwater valley about 1 mile away at a depth of 1000 feet. The enemy torpedoes won't be able to find us there."

"Deploy countermeasures and take us down to that valley. Nestle us in and rig for ultra-quiet."

"Aye, Captain. Deploying countermeasures," the XO responded. *Pasadena* launched two neutrally buoyant, barrel-shaped countermeasures. The size of 5-gallon buckets, each contained heat and noise generators designed to mimic a submarine's presence. They also emitted a large electromagnetic field and reflected active sonar signals, creating a convincing decoy.

Pasadena began a rapid descent to 1000 feet, aiming for the undersea valley.

Meanwhile, *Sea Dragon's* AI detected the counterattack. Her evasion protocol activated instantly. She released six ultra-maneuverable anti-torpedo countermeasures from small tubes near her bow. Each countermeasure, resembling a small air-to-air missile, utilized small thrusters to adjust its trajectory in the water. *Sea Dragon* dove as *Pasadena's* torpedoes closed in.

The countermeasures, equipped with ultra-sensitive passive sonar, locked onto the incoming threats. Calculating their bearings and speeds, they activated their thrusters and adjusted their fins. They spiraled through the water, converging on *Pasadena's* torpedoes and detonating on impact, neutralizing the threat.

Pasadena nestled into the undersea valley, waiting for *Sea Dragon's* torpedoes to engage the decoys above. The crew held their breath, listening to the faint echoes of explosions overhead. The countermeasures worked perfectly, drawing the enemy torpedoes away.

Captain Reese exhaled slowly. *Pasadena* had survived its first encounter with the PLA Navy's AI-powered submarine.

7

Tiger Claw

The voices grew louder. They stopped just outside the server room. Grace's pulse quickened. The program needed more time. And just then, she heard a large explosion reverberate through the ship. Immediately the sirens blared and the two guards ran to their action stations elsewhere in the ship. The EPX-2 charges had gone off, and *Tiger Claw* was taking on water.

The virus upload finished. With the worm deployed, it was time for Grace to get out. Grace reached under her uniform and slid out a small backpack. She pulled out a pair of goggles and slipped the computer in the bag. She flung the bag around her back and headed topside. She might attract some attention with a backpack on, but with the ship now taking on water and the crew in a panic, escape would be easy.

Grace ran up the stairwell to top deck. She looked over the port side of the ship, smoke and flames in the distance. *Tiger Claw* was a wounded animal at sea. If not for the sirens and yelling all around the ship, it would have been a beautiful, starry night at sea. Grace slipped the goggles over her eyes as she sprinted towards the edge of the ship and dove headfirst into the water some 30 feet below. The cold waters of the Pacific nipped her face and hands, but she was insulated by a thin wetsuit under her uniform.

She swam using the technique she had learned at the academy—using a special combat side-stroke, she was able to quietly swim away from the ship and bob her head up for breaths, even with the added weight of her backpack and handgun. After swimming for one mile, she reached for a square object hanging around her neck. She pressed it twice to activate her locator beacon. She looked back at the *Tiger Claw*—the flames coming from the ship still visible in the distance. She looked above and marveled at the stars.

Twenty minutes later, she heard something bubbling near the surface. That must be them. She swam towards the sound and hit a hard wall. It was the infiltrator sub. She took a deep breath and swam to the front hatch and found a keypad. She punched in the access code. The pre-flooded hatch opened and she swam inside, closing the hatch behind her.

In 10 seconds, the compartment was drained and oxygenated. Commander Jackson opened the inner hatch and greeted her. "Did you do it?"

"We're in," Grace replied, shivering. "Now, can someone hand me a towel and some hot coffee?"

8

Captain Lee had to bring *Tiger Claw* back to China for repairs after the explosion. It was not enough to sink *Tiger Claw* (flooded compartments were sealed off quickly), but she would have to stay close to the naval base until onboard repairs were finished. In the meantime, *Tiger Claw* was assigned the glorious duty of monitoring offshore weather patterns for the Navy. Ever patient, Lee knew that once repairs were finished he could head back to Japanese waters and hunt for the submarine that did this to him.

The *Tiger Claw's* central computer hummed away—a sleek piece of machinery designed for maximum speed and security. But even the strongest fortress had a weakness. And today, the *Tiger Claw* was not as invincible as its crew believed.

Hidden deep within the labyrinth of *Tiger Claw's* mainframe was *Whisper*, a worm so elegantly coded that it could slither through the vast maze of code and functions without being detected. Marvin had worked on it for weeks.

The worm had one primary mission: to intercept the keystore and its password during *Tiger Claw's* communication with *Sea Dragon. Tiger Claw* was often the designated flagship of the East Sea Fleet, so *Sea Dragon* was likely nearby.

As the clock neared 2300 hours, *Tiger Claw* initiated an authentication sequence with *Sea Dragon.* Streams of encrypted data flowed back and forth between the two entities—unbroken lines of ones and zeroes, a language the machines spoke fluently.

Inside the computer, the *Whisper* stirred. It recognized the specific pattern of data it was waiting for. Like a snake sensing the warmth of its prey, the worm slithered stealthily toward the authentication protocols, wrapping itself around the data stream.

In moments, the keystore and its password passed through. The *Whisper* lunged, silently copying the precious information, holding it within its coded coils.

Now came the tricky part—broadcasting this stolen data to the U.S. without alerting the CCP. The worm couldn't send out a full message; that would raise immediate alarms. It had to be subtle.

Recalling its coded instructions, the *Whisper* analyzed some of *Tiger Claw's* broadcasts. Using this, it piggybacked on the broadcast of a routine weather report being sent to a nearby CCP base. The stolen data was interlaced with the weather stats—temperatures, wave heights, and barometric pressures—making it look innocuous.

This camouflaged transmission would be sent over several channels, but among them was a specific frequency the U.S. intelligence was monitoring closely. To the untrained eye or any other scanner, it would appear as a simple weather update. But the U.S. was looking specifically for a pattern from *Whisper*.

The worm waited patiently as the report began its transmission. As the data flowed out, the *Whisper* gently pushed the stolen information onto the known USA channel, careful to maintain its cover behind a mundane weather forecast.

American destroyer USS *Guardian* was navigating a shipping lane just a few hundred miles away in international waters. A young operator adjusted her headset, her eyes narrowing as she focused on the incoming transmission. "Sir," she called out to the captain. "I think we've got something."

Back on the *Tiger Claw*, the authentication with the *Sea Dragon* completed smoothly. There were no alerts, no indication of any security breaches. The CCP destroyer continued its mission, unaware that its most prized secret had just been broadcasted into enemy hands.

And deep within its central computer, the *Whisper* worm deleted itself, erasing any trace of its activity like it never existed.

An ensign entered the bridge of *Tiger Claw*. "Captain," he said, "repairs have finished and all systems are operational."

"Excellent," replied Captain Lee. "Chart a course back to Japan. It's time to pay our friends a visit."

Part Six

Quantum Vengeance

1

Naval Station, Pearl Harbor

Pasadena docked in Hawaii for inspection after its tussle with *Sea Dragon*. Because they might need to redeploy with *Pasadena* soon, Marvin and Grace had to stay nearby. The two CIA agents enjoyed the tropical paradise, but they felt a general uneasiness knowing that an AI-powered nuclear submarine lurked somewhere in the Pacific, waiting to pounce on any American submarine or ship that ventured too close.

It was a clear, sunny day. Marvin and Grace sat on beach chairs on the white sand, facing the setting sun over the Pacific. Officially off duty, they blended in perfectly as tourists on the beach. Grace sported an emerald green two-piece bikini, and Marvin was shirtless with blue swim trunks. It was only seven months ago that Marvin had met Grace through InstaVR, and he still found her extremely attractive. Her bikini and flawless curves weren't making things any easier.

"Doesn't it feel weird?" Marvin asked, trying really hard not to stare at Grace's hourglass figure. "The world is on the brink of nuclear war and we're sipping drinks here on the beach."

"If I've learned one thing in this profession Marvin, it's that you should take advantage of moments like these to relax a bit." Grace turned her head towards Marvin and raised her sunglasses, looking Marvin in the eye. "You never know how long the next deployment will be, or if you'll even make it back alive. So, soak up some sun and enjoy yourself a bit. We've earned a break."

"Yeah, maybe you're right." Marvin said as he admired how the yellow and orange sunbeams played with Grace's dark, voluminous hair. He shook the thought out of his head—he really had to focus on the mission. "Cheers," he said as he raised his mint mojito. Grace raised her cocktail, and they both took a sip and enjoyed the ocean breeze.

Marvin listened to the sound of the ocean waves washing up on shore, the sound of children laughing and playing in the water, the birds chirping. The public had heard about the attack in Japan through the news, but that seemed like a whole world away. Most people just wanted to live in blissful ignorance of the commotion abroad. America was safe, they thought. What happens in Asia or whoever China bombed wasn't a concern to most. America had its nuclear arsenal, and nobody threatened its shores.

Grace's phone rang. "We spoke too soon Marvin, looks like Langley's calling."

"Hello, Grace here." She started intently out into space as she listened to the call. "Makes sense Director, understood."

"Marvin," she said as she hung up. "Grab your stuff. We're back in the fight!"

2

Langley, Virginia

Director Lin dialed an encrypted line and listened for the voice of Japan's Minister of Foreign Affairs, Noboru Yoshida. He hoped Yoshida would be open to cooperation with the US in light of the recent nuclear attack.

The phone buzzed to life. "Yoshida speaking."

"Minister," Lin began, a solemn note in his voice, "I trust you remember the *Tiger Claw*?"

"How could I forget?" Yoshida exclaimed. "That ship and their hidden submarine wreaked havoc on our fleet. The audacity of the Chinese to deploy such power against us!"

Director Lin continued, "Our intelligence has located *Tiger Claw* south of Japan. I have a proposal to bring them back into your waters. Into Tokyo Bay."

Yoshida's voice wavered. "Why would I want that monster near our shores again?"

"China dropped a nuclear weapon on your nation. Japan deserves closure."

"What's your plan, Director?"

"The US Navy has taken a covert step. We fired two torpedoes at the *Tiger Claw* last month. They'll be looking for the submarine responsible. If you tell Admiral Chen the attacking submarine might be docked in Tokyo Bay, the *Tiger Claw* may return for retaliation."

Yoshida took a moment to process this. "You're using us as bait. But what if the Chinese attack again, in revenge? Or if they discover there is no submarine, and this is all a ruse?"

Director Lin replied, "The US will help Japan. And *Tiger Claw* will not leave Tokyo Bay. You have my word."

Silence echoed on the line. Lin could almost hear the gears turning in Yoshida's mind.

"How high does this go?" Yoshida asked.

"My orders come from the President," Lin said. "And we never had this conversation."

After a brief pause, Yoshida responded, "Alright. We'll lure *Tiger Claw* back to Tokyo Bay. And unofficially, China's recent actions against us have made Japan more open to Western cooperation. Officially we remain neutral, but let this be the start of a new chapter between our two countries."

"Understood, Minister," Lin replied.

Lin hung up the phone. The game of geopolitics was ever-changing, but in this moment, the fate of the East hung in the balance, with Tokyo Bay set to be its epicenter.

Yoshida dialed General Nakamura, the Chief of Staff for the Japan Self Defense Force. "General," Yoshida said. "I want to talk to you about our response to China's nuclear attack on Osaka."

3

Ministry of Foreign Affairs, Tokyo

The dark room was bathed in soft amber light. Noboru Yoshida sat behind a large mahogany desk, waiting for his desk phone to connect.

After a few moments, a crisp voice emerged from the other side. It was Admiral Chen.

"Admiral," Yoshida began, acting cordial. "It's Noboru Yoshida. I hope you are well."

"Minister Yoshida. This is unexpected. To what do I owe the pleasure?"

Yoshida cleared his throat, searching for the right words. "Admiral, I am reaching out in the spirit of the defensive alliance between our two nations. My hope is to share some critical intelligence that might be of interest to you."

There was a brief pause. "Go on."

"Your *Tiger Claw* was attacked by a submarine recently," Yoshida continued, "I regret to inform you that the submarine in question is Japanese."

"Are you saying your own people were behind this?" Chen asked, surprised.

"Not the Japanese government, but a renegade faction within our navy. The captain of the submarine is a staunch nationalist with influential family ties. Our attempts to rein him in have been futile, due to his connections. He's become something of a wildcard, and it's making many in our circles nervous."

Chen took a moment, absorbing this. "Why tell me this, Minister? This sounds like an internal matter."

Yoshida kept calm to avoid revealing his deception. "Because, Admiral, in two weeks, that very submarine is scheduled to dock in Tokyo Harbor for repairs. I believe this might present the PLA Navy with an opportunity to neutralize this threat once and for all. We could, of course, handle this ourselves, but we wanted to extend this opportunity to you as a gesture of goodwill."

A heavy silence hung in the air, before Chen replied, "You are offering us a submarine, and its captain, on a silver platter?"

"Yes, Admiral. It's a risk for us. But it's the right thing to do, to ensure the longevity of our partnership."

"Very well, Minister," replied Chen. "I appreciate your transparency. Rest assured, we will handle this matter."

Yoshida breathed a sigh of relief. "Thank you, Admiral. Let this be a testament to Japan's dedication to our alliance."

4

Tiger Claw

Admiral Chen sat contemplatively in his stateroom, the silence around him a stark contrast to the storm of thoughts swirling in his mind. He reached his room phone, dialing the bridge with a practiced swiftness. The line beeped a terse rhythm before Captain Lee answered.

"This is the captain," Lee's voice came through, crisp and professional.

Without preamble, Chen delved into the heart of the matter. "I've just received intelligence from Minister Yoshida that our rogue submarine will be docked in Tokyo Harbor in two weeks for repairs. This might be our chance," he disclosed, the significance of the information hanging heavily between them.

Lee's response was immediate, his interest sharpened by the news. "You trust this information, Admiral? What if it's a trap?"

"It came directly from Yoshida," Chen assured, though his voice carried an undercurrent of doubt. "He claims it's a gesture of good faith. But we need to be cautious. We'll bring *Sea Dragon*."

Lee paused. "We need *Sea Dragon* for this?" he questioned, the implications of deploying such a formidable asset not lost on him.

"I don't want to take any chances," replied Chen. "If this rogue submarine somehow evades the *Tiger Claw*, *Sea Dragon* will ensure it doesn't slip away."

"Understood, Admiral. We won't let them escape," Lee affirmed.

Chen lingered on the line, the silence stretching between them as he grappled with the enormity of their undertaking. "Lee, this isn't just about the submarine," he finally said, his tone somber. "This is about setting a precedent. Showing the world that no one, not even a rogue nation or faction, can challenge the might of the PLA Navy."

"The message will be loud and clear, Admiral."

Chen hung up the receiver. He headed to the ship's deck where he watched the setting sun paint the sky in shades of burning orange and fading pink.

The trust placed in Minister Yoshida's intelligence was a gamble, but Chen knew that in the shadowy realms of espionage and international diplomacy, risk was unavoidable. The deal with Yoshida represented a convergence of interests, and Chen remained acutely aware of the potential for betrayal. But he was confident in *Tiger Claw,* especially with the force multiplier of *Sea Dragon* nearby.

The sun dipped below the horizon, and the world was bathed in twilight. *Tiger Claw* and *Sea Dragon* began their hunt for the rogue Japanese submarine.

5

Somewhere in the Pacific

Marvin and Grace crowded around the executive table in the officer's briefing room of the *Pasadena*. The room, typically a place of strategic planning and calculated discussions, felt unusually charged today. Captain Reese's grave tone set the stage for a mission unlike any they had encountered before.

"This next mission makes the last one look like a training exercise," Captain Reese stated, his gaze sweeping across the room. His usual composure was tinged with a clear note of disapproval. "I don't like it one bit, but our hands are tied. The masterminds at Langley have left us with no alternative. Nonetheless, we're here to ensure your safe return. Commander Jackson, you have the floor."

SEAL Commander Jackson got up from his seat. He approached the map centered on Tokyo Bay with a laser pointer in hand, highlighting the geographical and strategic complexities of their mission.

"Intelligence shows that the PLA has set up a communications tower in Yokohama, which is an ideal spot to spy on Tokyo and Tokyo Bay. The tower is capable of spying on all signals in the region, and it can also jam enemy frequencies. From the outside, it looks like a two story office building with some radio antennae on top—they're fronting it as a commercial broadcasting company. But we've positively identified PLA soldiers at the site. There are at least two radio operators, and at least six PLA soldiers in the building. Because they are operating under the guise of a real business, they don't have any armed guards outside of the building. But we've seen weapons being offloaded from trucks into the building, so we know they're packing heat.

"*Pasadena* will bring us about 10 miles off the coast, in Sagami Bay. From there, we'll depart in the infiltration sub and cruise for about an hour before we surface at an abandoned shipping dock. Fortunately for us, the dock is covered so it will mask our activities from any spy satellites. We get out, unload our gear, and then connect with a local transport at point Alpha."

Marvin, absorbing every detail, finally voiced the question on everyone's mind. "Who's going, exactly?"

Commander Jackson, pointing to the map, outlined the infiltration path, emphasizing the critical nature of Marvin's role. "My SEALs and I will ensure you get inside that tower. You need to be prepared to execute the next phase—intercepting communications between hostile forces. Your expertise is vital."

"And I'm coming too," Grace chimed in. "I can't let you boys have all the fun, can I?"

Her comment elicited a brief chuckle in the room, breaking the intensity of their planning. "Right," Jackson acknowledged, with a nod of respect towards Grace. "Your contributions on the *Tiger Claw* mission were invaluable. We're happy to have you on the ground with us."

The team concluded the briefing. "Let's head to the ready room and gear up," Jackson said.

The team dispersed, moving to the ready room—a place brimming with activity and the final steps of mission prep. Marvin and Grace, alongside Commander Jackson and the SEALs, meticulously checked their equipment.

As they packed their equipment, the reality of the mission settled in. Marvin, adjusting the straps of his backpack, realized this would be his first deployment into hostile territory. Grace, checking her own gear, offered a reassuring smile. "We've got this, Marvin. We've trained for it, and we're not alone."

Commander Jackson, overhearing their exchange, added, "It's not just about getting in and out. It's about making sure we all come back together. Keep your heads on a swivel and we'll all come home alive."

6

Yokohama

The infiltration submarine surfaced by the abandoned shipping dock. Marvin, Grace, and five SEALs climbed out. A cold metal warehouse covered their moves from prying satellites or drones. They brought a few crates of ammunition and weapons out of the sub and prepared for their mission.

They suited up with new TitanX armor, a special ballistic suit with special layers of high density polymer, designed to stop most armor piercing rounds while being 10X lighter than traditional armors. With the TitanX suit, a soldier only added 10 pounds of weight and protected about 80% of his body. Weak points were around the joints and neck areas, but the center of mass and limbs were well protected.

After suiting up, Marvin grabbed a TitanX Helmet. It was a thin wrap-around helmet providing excellent ballistic protection, and it featured a bulletproof glass visor with a heads-up display. As the user moved around, the visor highlighted targets onscreen and colored areas of interest. In night-vision mode, it displayed an illuminated 3D model of the environment which meshed perfectly with the real world.

Marvin grabbed a familiar weapon, the 7.62mm E-Coil rifle. It was exactly like the model he trained with during bootcamp, except this time loaded with a magazine of 60 armor piercing rounds. He quickly checked the battery and muzzle velocity settings—100% charge, and 1000 FPS. Marvin's helmet display synchronized with his rifle, so he could see how many rounds remained in his magazine at all times.

The team snuck out the back of the warehouse and trekked about 100 yards west to find their transportation —a nondescript shipping truck that had been placed there by local operatives the night before. Yokohama was 30 minutes away by car. Commander Jackson pushed the starter button and the fuel-cell powered van came to life.

It was midnight. As they approached the target destination, Marvin glanced out the front of the van and saw the metallic frame of the radio tower about 200 yards ahead. Nestled close to Tokyo harbor, the radio tower blended in well with the backdrop of the busy Tokyo urban jungle. "Time to go," Jackson said as he stopped the van behind some trees.

Marvin felt tense. This was the first time he was deploying with live weapons as part of an assault team. This was not a beginner mission.

"Remember what we discussed," Grace said to Marvin before they got out of the van. "You're a specialist on this mission. The VIP. Stick to the back of our stack, and don't engage the enemy unless you're in immediate danger. I don't want you in the fight. You leave that to us. Stay alive, and get to the central computer at all costs."

Grace placed her hand on Marvin's shoulder and looked into his eyes. "This is what we trained for. You'll do great."

Grace hopped out of the van, and Marvin took a deep breath and followed her. The assault had begun.

The SEALs led Marvin and Grace through back alleys to get to the tower. Normally, Japan was busy at night, but the radio tower was situated in a remote and industrial park area. It was a ghost town after 6 PM, but the team still had to be vigilant.

"Okay Marvin," said Commander Jackson. "We're about 50 yards to the radio tower. Deploy your jammer here."

Marvin's backpack held a laptop and a black box with a numeric keypad on it. Marvin grabbed the black box and punched in the activation code, and then hid the box behind a dumpster nearby. The box emitted a powerful jamming signal that blocked long range radio transmissions for a 100 yard radius. This jamming would alert the enemy that something was amiss, but they wouldn't be able to call for help.

"We've only got 30 minutes before the jammer runs out of power," said Marvin. "The jammer is deployed."

The team identified the broadcasting building—a nondescript brick building about 50' x 50' with two floors. It had dark tinted windows, and was only faintly illuminated on the outside. Security cameras at each corner kept careful watch for any interlocutors.

"We need a clear approach to the backdoor," said Jackson. "I'm deploying the EMP drone."

Jackson unzipped a satchel attached to his hip and brought out a small helicopter drone. He pushed a few buttons and it buzzed to life, and it synchronized with his helmet display so he could see everything the drone could see. He used hand gestures to navigate the drone up over the security cameras, and proceeded to zap each camera with a burst of EMP energy from the drone. The drone was only capable of five minutes of operation, so he had to be fast. And the EMP only disabled each camera for 10 minutes.

"All cameras disabled, let's move!" said Jackson. "Phillips, boobytrap the door and meet us out back."

Officer Phillips ran up to the front door of the building and grabbed a red disk from his chest rig. He squeezed the disk and pressed the center, arming it. Removing a plastic sheet off the back to reveal an adhesive cover, he gently placed it on the front door. The disk had enough explosive potential to destroy the door and kill anyone within a 10 foot radius. Phillips backed off from the door and quickly wrapped around the building to meet the team at the back door.

"Split the stack on this door," whispered Jackson. The SEALs formed two lines on the left and right sides of the door. "Michaels, wand it."

Officer Michaels quietly grabbed a rifle-like device from the back of his suit. This was a special optical wand that used a flexible wire camera to see under doors. He extended the wand under the door and looked around. "Long hallway, two contacts walking towards door—armed. Ten seconds." The guards were likely coming to investigate what had disrupted their security cameras.

"Blow the door, frag, and clear," said Jackson.

Officer Michaels quickly pulled a metal disk from his hip pouch. He pushed three buttons in order and the disk blinked to life. He attached it to the center of the door and pulled out his detonator, a small handheld transmitter that needed to be squeezed. "Ready," he said.

Jackson pulled the pin out of his frag grenade. "Do it," he said.

Michaels quickly squeezed the transmitter several times, and the disk exploded in a bright flash, vaporizing the door and stunning the two guards on the other side. Jackson threw the frag in and then readied his rifle as he mentally counted down. "3… 2… 1…" BOOM.

The grenade sent shrapnel into the two guards, killing them instantly. Phillips charged into the room with Jackson and the others quickly following. They would need to clear the rest of the building without the element of surprise—the whole building probably heard the blast.

The SEALs walked in a two column formation down the hallway. A guard heard the blast and came rushing out of the bathroom on the left. Jackson greeted him with a hail of gunfire, dropping him immediately. "I'm going in!" said Jackson as he kicked down the door and cleared the bathroom. Two SEALs remained at the door to cover, and one followed him in to help clear the bathroom.

"Bathroom clear," Jackson reported.

Marvin and Grace waited for one of the SEALs to shout, "All clear!" Grace headed into the hallway and Marvin quickly followed. They caught up to the team at the midpoint of the hallway, and together proceeded to the far door. Marvin tried not to look at the blood splattered around the floor.

"Three guards down," he thought. "That means there are at least three more in this building."

They formed a split stack at the far end of the hallway by the door. They heard a panicked commotion in the next room, people shouting orders in Mandarin and rearranging furniture.

"Frag and clear!" shouted Jackson to his team. He readied another frag, and Phillips pushed the door open. Jackson tossed in the frag just as before and counted down. BOOM.

Phillips charged in but was met with a hail of gunfire.

The PLA soldiers had set up a rotary cannon and were firing 7.62mm armor piercing rounds at over 5000 rounds per minute. The bullets whizzed through the doorway and pierced through the walls. Jackson and Phillips were cut down by a flurry of rounds piercing through their TitanX suits like needles through paper. The gunner swept his aim sideways and hit the two remaining SEALs by the door.

Marvin and Grace dove to the ground and barely avoided the flurry. "Retreat, Marvin!" shouted Grace. "Head to the bathroom and stay low!" Grace popped a smoke grenade and tossed it into the main room, at least providing some concealment for the two as they retreated to the bathroom.

"Fuck!" Grace said, breathing heavily. "The intelligence team must have missed the goddamn part where they shipped in a rotary cannon. I think… I think our team's dead."

"What do we do?" Asked Marvin. "We have to get to the control room."

"I know. Let me think."

Grace remembered the front door was still boobytrapped with a motion detonator.

"I'm going out the back. I'll try to breach the front. The next room is the main lobby. I might be able to flank them."

"What should I do?"

"You stay put, and keep your rifle trained on the door in case anyone tries to come in here. Marvin, you absolutely need to get to the control room. I'll radio when all clear."

Grace's helmet display flickered. She took off her helmet and inspected it, and realized a bullet had gone through part of it—it wasn't deep enough to hit her skull, but the round had broken the circuitry inside.

"Great, my helmet's busted. I guess we won't have radio. We're doing this the old-fashioned way. If you don't hear from me in 10 minutes, assume the worst and press on. It will all be up to you."

Grace grabbed her last smoke grenade and lobbed it down the hallway. It popped and let out a huge black cloud of smoke, and she sprinted towards the rear exit. Marvin sat with his back to the wall, and his rifle trained on the bathroom entrance. He hoped nobody would come through—he'd never shot anyone before.

Grace sprinted around the building and approached the front door. The boobytrap was still intact. Miraculously, nobody had tried to open the door yet. She walked up to the door and put her Mandarin to good use.

"This is Officer Chen of the PLA," she shouted. "We received your distress call and are here to reinforce you. Open the door!"

She heard one of the guards inside. “It’s about time! We’ve lost a lot of men!”

Grace retreated from the door and readied her rifle. The guard released the door bolt and turned the doorknob. Beep. The motion-activated detonator triggered the explosive, tearing through the steel door and launching the guard 20 feet back into the room. The blast killed him instantly.

Grace lobbed a frag grenade into the room. BOOM! She rushed in with her rifle ready and shot the rotary cannon operator three times. Just as she lowered her rifle, she remembered that she hadn’t checked the left corner of the room…

POW. She spun and emptied her magazine into the corner as she fell down with a shout of pain. A stinging sensation gripped her, she glanced down and saw she had taken a shot to her side near the abdomen. She was bleeding profusely. She had been hit by a high velocity armor piercing round.

Marvin had heard everything. The front door explosion, the frag grenade, and the firefight. He also heard Grace scream out in pain, and didn’t hear anything else after that. “I need to go in!” he thought.

Marvin took a deep breath and prepared to exit into the hallway. He’d have to check carefully to make sure the rotary cannon was neutralized first. He leaned out into the hallway and used the camera on his rifle to zoom in on the far doorway. He saw the rotary cannon, unmanned. It seemed like Grace had cleared the room. He hugged the wall and headed towards the lobby.

As he approached the doorway, he went cold. He saw Grace, unconscious or dead, laying in a pool of blood. “No, Grace!” He rushed into the room.

He was so focused on Grace that he forgot PIE the door before entering the room. He didn't see the PLA soldier standing to the side of the door, waiting in ambush. The soldier grabbed Marvin's rifle and performed a sweeping move with his feet to knock Marvin to the ground.

As they wrestled for the rifle, Marvin made a quick decision to slip under his rifle strap and let the soldier take the gun. The soldier grabbed the gun and turned it back towards Marvin. Click. Nothing happened. The E-Coil rifle had been coded to a special near-field sensor in the palm of Marvin's TitanX armor. It couldn't be fired by anyone but Marvin.

Marvin charged towards the soldier and wrapped his arms around the soldier's waist, and stepped behind him to perform a takedown. The soldier fell down with Marvin and they fought for dominance on the floor. Marvin used his weight to pin down the soldier and then climbed on top of him. The soldier, laying face up on the ground, struggled to get up but Marvin slammed his elbow down into the soldier's forehead. Blood trickled into the soldier's eyes as he screamed and turned his body to hide his face away from Marvin. Marvin, now on the soldier's back, sprawled out and wrapped his legs around the soldier's knees and then reached his arm under the soldier's neck to form a chokehold.

But the thickness of the TitanX armor on Marvin's arm made it nearly impossible to perform a proper chokehold. Marvin realized this after about 10 seconds of struggle. Using his free hand, he unsheathed a 4-inch push knife from his utility belt. Keeping the soldier in the chokehold, Marvin brought the knife up to the exposed side of the soldier's neck and pushed hard. The soldier screamed as the knife cut into flesh. Marvin felt the knife connect with bone, and he shoved the knife into the vertebrae as hard as he could. Blood splattered everywhere. The guard gurgled up blood and his body went limp. Marvin rolled off of the lifeless body beneath him. It was his first kill.

Time had slowed down for Marvin. He was still riding the adrenaline rush of the fight. But then he remembered Grace and snapped back to reality.

He ran over to her. “Grace, wake up!” His voice was both a plea and a command, laden with desperation. Gently, he slipped an arm under her knees and another behind her back, lifting her just enough to drag her body closer to the nearby wall.

As he maneuvered her into a sitting position against the wall, Marvin assessed her injuries. It didn’t look good.

Grace opened her eyes, barely there. “Marvin… You need to get to the control room. You need to complete the mission…” She coughed up some blood. “It’s upstairs. Give me a handgun, I’ll watch the stairwell…”

Grace lost consciousness. Marvin fought back the tears and reminded himself that this was not the time to get emotional. But he remembered all the evenings he had spent with Grace in San Francisco, the chats they had while training at Langley… Her sardonic humor, her wit, and her smile.

He realized this might be the last time he ever saw her alive. But he didn’t have time to linger. “Thank you for everything Grace,” he said, placing his hand on her forehead and wiping away some of the blood and dirt. He grabbed a compression bandage from his utility belt and wrapped it around Grace’s abdomen to slow the bleeding. He took one last look at her, picked up his rifle, and faced the stairwell.

Something had changed in him. He no longer feared death. He wanted revenge.

Marvin proceeded up the stairs. He knew there might be enemies on the second floor, so he had to clear it all himself. He kept his rifle focused on the top of the stairwell as he cautiously moved upstairs. He saw a hallway with two doors on the left, and one door on the right.

He suspected the two doors on the left were the main control room, so he'd clear the room on the right first. He approached the door on the knob side. He gave the knob a twist and pushed the door forward, then backed up to start his PIE of the room. He did it quickly, then aimed his rifle to check the center of the room. He stepped in and checked the right corner. It was an empty server room. He went inside and quickly checked behind the servers—all clear.

Marvin headed back to the hallway and stacked up on the knob side of one of the doors to the control room. This one would be tough, since there were likely to be multiple enemies inside. He didn't know if they were armed. And he couldn't throw a frag grenade into this room because it could damage the central computer. He had to do this the old fashioned way. And he'd have to do it fast.

He heard voices inside. It sounded like the radiomen were panicked and trying to get in contact with nearby PLA assets. He checked his watch—only two minutes left until his radio jammer ran out of battery power. The radiomen could call for reinforcements soon.

Marvin quietly checked the doorknob. Locked. Marvin took a deep breath, pointed his gun at the doorknob, and fired 3 rounds. BAM BAM BAM! The doorknob vaporized and Marvin kicked the door in with his right leg and sprinted into the room. He swept his rifle from left to right as quickly as he could. One radioman, sitting at the central computer, was caught off guard. He turned towards Marvin and reached for a sidearm, but Marvin fired off three rounds into his chest. He went down. The other radioman bolted towards the other door in an attempt to escape. Marvin peppered the radioman with a dozen rounds, and he went down. All clear.

He ran over to the central computer. He reached into his backpack and pulled out a laptop and slicer cable, and attached it to the computer's hub. He ran a program to install a backdoor into the system and accessed a secure shell. He found the broadcasting program and provided *Tiger Claw's* keystore and password, and he loaded *Tiger Claw's* information into the system. With *Tiger Claw's* public and private keys, he could decrypt any broadcast from *Tiger Claw,* and extract any symmetric keys exchanged between *Tiger Claw* and *Sea Dragon* after their authentication handshake. Then they could encrypt and decrypt messages using the intercepted symmetric key, effectively mimicking *Tiger Claw*'s authentic communications with *Sea Dragon.*

He checked the time. His radio jammer had switched off by now. He could send and receive radio broadcasts!

7

USS Pasadena

Captain Reese scanned the glowing monitors before him, eyes darting to the sonar readings. The submarine had nestled itself deep in an undersea valley about 80 miles from Tokyo Bay, using the natural contours of the ocean floor as a protective cloak from sonar.

Ensign Clarke sat at the sonar station. "*Tiger Claw* is pinging," he reported. "Active sonar."

Captain Reese leaned forward slightly, his voice steady. "Where is it?"

"The target is 10 miles from the entrance to Tokyo Bay," Clarke responded.

Tiger Claw was on the hunt. *Pasadena,* an SSN(X) class submarine, was coated in a sonar-absorbing stealth polymer. But *Pasadena* still needed to be careful.

"Continue passive sonar. Monitor *Tiger Claw's* progress," Captain Reese ordered. The *Pasadena* would not give away its position, relying instead on its passive listening devices to track the movements of its adversaries.

Captain Reese walked to the sonar console. "Clarke, any sign of *Sea Dragon*?"

The ensign shook his head. "No. That's the troubling part. *Pasadena's* passive sonar is among the best, and yet we can't hear it. Either it's too far, or it's operating at a level of stealth we've not encountered before."

Reese frowned. "So, we're blind to it?"

Clarke nodded. "For now, at least."

As the minutes ticked by, *Tiger Claw's* sonar pings became less frequent until they ceased completely. The crew of the *Pasadena* could hear the destroyer's engines wind down, a sign that the destroyer neared the harbor.

"Now's our chance," Reese murmured. "Helmsman, bring us up to 50 feet. Rig for ultra quiet."

"Aye, Captain," came the swift response.

Pasadena began its silent ascent, taking care to minimize noise. At 50 feet, they would be invisible to any surface ship but could fire a salvo of missiles while submerged.

Ensign Clarke, still glued to the sonar display, reported, "*Tiger Claw* has entered the mouth of Tokyo Bay, Captain. They've stopped their active sonar."

Reese allowed himself a small smile. "Good. We move when they're distracted with the decoy in the harbor. That's when we'll have our best shot."

Just then, a low hum emanated from the sonar station, barely perceptible but there. It was different from the *Tiger Claw's* rumbling propellers, more refined.

Clarke's eyes widened slightly. "Captain, I think... I think that's the *Sea Dragon.* It's distant, but the signature... it matches no known sub, but the pattern is definitely submerged. It's incredibly faint, but it's there."

"Can you get a fix on its position?" Asked Reese.

Clarke hesitated, recalibrating the instruments. "It's difficult, Captain. The readings are inconsistent. It might be employing some form of acoustic masking. We just know there's something out there. We just can't pin down the location."

Reese looked thoughtful for a moment. The *Sea Dragon*, the AI-driven submarine, was an enigma—silent, unpredictable, and deadly. "We stay on course. Monitor for *Sea Dragon*, but our primary target remains the *Tiger Claw*. We'll deal with the *Sea Dragon* when the time comes."

Clarke looked uneasy. "Sir, the *Sea Dragon* is an unknown. We don't truly know what it's capable of."

Reese met his gaze, his eyes steely. "That's why we must remain unpredictable. The Dragon might be AI-driven, but it hasn't encountered many SSN(X) submarines before. We have the element of surprise, and we need to use it."

Clarke nodded, "Understood, Captain."

The minutes ticked by slowly. The crew of *Pasadena*, seasoned by countless missions, knew the importance of patience and precision.

Finally, Captain Reese broke the silence. "XO, prepare 16 Harpoon-X missiles. We make our move soon. Program them to prioritize the radio and radar elements of *Tiger Claw*."

Executive officer Smith responded, "Arming missiles and programming a firing solution, Captain."

As the crew readied itself for what might be the most critical mission of its tenure, Reese took a moment to reflect. In this vast, dark expanse of the ocean, the game of cat and mouse continued, but with stakes higher than ever before. The *Pasadena* was about to make its mark, but the shadows held secrets, and she knew *Sea Dragon* was out there. As soon as they launched their missiles, *Sea Dragon* would come for them.

8

Captain Lee stood on the command bridge of the *Tiger Claw*, his gaze focused intently on the mouth of Tokyo Bay which glowed faintly behind a thick layer of fog. Every fiber of his being was primed for a confrontation. With Admiral Chen standing nearby observing his every move, he felt the pressure of the moment weigh on him. He would certainly receive a promotion after this mission, he thought.

The XO handed Lee a phone receiver. "Message, Captain," the XO said.

"Captain, we are receiving a transmission from a Japanese submarine docked in Tokyo Bay," said the officer on the other end of the line.

"Send it through on speaker," said Captain Lee. An officer pressed a few buttons and the transmission cackled through the bridge speakers. "This is Captain Watanabe of the JS *Kaizen*. Identify your intentions in Tokyo Bay."

Lee's lips curled into a smirk. The audacity of Watanabe to hail him directly was a surprise, but he had been waiting for this confrontation.

"We have unfinished business, Watanabe," Lee responded coolly. "Your submarine attacked the *Tiger Claw*. It's time to answer for your transgression."

The line was quiet for a moment. When Watanabe finally responded, his voice was laced with confusion. "There must be some mistake. The *Kaizen* has no quarrel with *Tiger Claw*. We've never attacked your ship."

But each denial only fanned the flames of Lee's conviction. "You think I'd fall for your lies, Watanabe? Every action has consequences, and yours are long overdue."

Hidden just 50 feet below the surface 80 miles away, the *Pasadena* and its crew waited, a tense atmosphere thickening the air in the submarine's control room.

Pasadena had a simple mission: Fire the payload and get out. Reese observed the display near the captain's chair. The screen showed the last known location of the *Tiger Claw* in Tokyo Bay.

Captain Reese glanced at his officers and contemplated his next move. "We've been given a golden opportunity," he murmured. "Bring up the periscope and prepare for launch."

"Aye Captain, raising the periscope," replied the XO.

Reese inhaled deeply, every sinew of his body taut with anticipation. "Confirm GPS coordinates and ready the launch sequence for 16 Harpoon-X anti-ship missiles," he commanded. "And ready a salvo of four X-48 torpedoes in sentinel mode to cover our escape. We will commence torpedo and missile launching simultaneously."

A symphony of beeps and clicks filled the control room as the crew prepped the ship's arsenal. The submarine hovered just below the surface, and a small sensor array peeked out of the water to help the submarine confirm its location. The sub's topside silo doors slid open, revealing the lethal cargo nestled within. The sub's frontside torpedo doors slid open as well.

"Launch on my command in 3...2...1..." Reese said. "Launch!"

With a sudden jolt, the first Harpoon-X jumped out of its launch tube with a burst of pressurized steam. The missile shot upwards, breaching the ocean's surface before its rocket booster ignited. It surged into the sky, leaving a gray contrail in its wake. Then at half-second intervals, an additional 15 additional missiles fired off. Guided by onboard AI, the missiles split into different trajectories, heading towards *Tiger Claw*. Each Harpoon-X contained a night-vision camera, active and passive radar, an inertial guidance system, and a radio transmitter. Using computer vision and a 3D model of *Tiger Claw*, each Harpoon-X could pinpoint the *Tiger Claw* exactly. They flew low over the ocean to avoid anti-missile defenses. Each missile was precise enough to hit a hummingbird in midair.

In parallel, *Pasadena* fired off four X-48 torpedoes. The torpedoes quietly sailed through the water and began a circular swim pattern after traveling for a mile. In sentinel mode, each torpedo used passive radar to identify any enemy submarine in the area. If it found a target, it would turn on active sonar and engage "pit bull" mode—chasing down its target at 50 knots. It was unlikely for an advanced submarine like *Sea Dragon* to walk into this trap, but the sentinel torpedoes at least discouraged direct pursuit from the rear. *Pasadena* lowered its periscope, descended to 500 feet, and fled at flank speed.

Sea Dragon was submerged near Tokyo Bay, communicating with *Tiger Claw* through a wired communications buoy that floated at the surface. It heard *Pasadena's* launch sequence and received a broadcast from *Tiger Claw* shortly after. *Sea Dragon* plotted a course as she reeled in her communications buoy, and she headed towards *Pasadena's* last known location at flank speed.

9

Aboard *Tiger Claw*, alarms blared, signaling incoming projectiles. Lee's face turned ashen. "Incoming missiles! I count 16 low flyers, off the starboard side!" shouted the radar officer.

"Deploy anti-air countermeasures! Time to impact?" responded Lee.

"Sir, impact in approximately 60 seconds!"

Traveling at Mach 3, *Pasadena's* Harpoon-X missiles could travel approximately one kilometer per second. Sailors scrambled on deck to brace for impact, and the Tiger Claw's anti-missile 30mm rotary cannons spun up, ready to shoot 6000 rounds per minute. Tiger Claw also powered up its anti-missile laser defense system; a 1 megawatt laser emitter mounted on the ship's conning tower. These rotary cannons were only effective up to 3 kilometers, but the laser could take out targets as far as 5 kilometers. Would they be able to stop all of the missiles in time? The laser required about a half second to destroy a missile, but its performance was severely degraded in poor weather or fog. And it was a particularly foggy night.

Tiger Claw fired off a salvo of 24 HQ-10Z surface-to-air missiles in quick succession. Each missile could approach Mach 3 and possessed infrared and passive homing, and could intercept supersonic targets between 3-10 kilometers away.

Onboard the lead Harpoon-X, active radar showed the anti-missile launches from the *Tiger Claw*. Each Harpoon-X utilized a hive mind connection to share information. Together, the Harpoon-X hive mind evaluated options and settled upon a strategy. Just 10 kilometers away from *Tiger Claw*, all but one of them turned off active radar and steered to different trajectories. Some went high, some stayed low. A single Harpoon-X continued forward, signaling its location loudly to the incoming HQ-10Zs by amplifying its active radar. As the first HQ-10Z approached, the Harpoon-X detonated into a massive fireball 10 meters wide. The temperature of the fireball reached 3000 degrees Celsius and quickly caught the attention of the heat-seeking HQ-10Zs.

The remaining 15 Harpoon-Xs continued along their paths towards *Tiger Claw*. By the time the HQ-10Zs realized they had locked on to the wrong target, the Harpoon-X swarm had already passed. Running low on fuel, the HQ-10Zs could not turn and pursue. One by one, they fizzled out and fell into the ocean.

Tiger Claw's fate now lay in the autonomous system driving the rotary cannons at the front and rear of the ship, as well as the anti-air laser on the ship's radar tower. The Harpoon-X swarm had spread out, with some missiles approaching low and some almost directly above *Tiger Claw*. The autonomous system focused its fire off the starboard side of the ship. There were only 3 seconds before impact.

The loud buzzing of machine gun fire echoed through the night. Tracer rounds could be seen for miles snaking out into the sky, with small detonations for each Harpoon-X shot down. The onboard laser attempted to lock and melt the missiles out of the sky, but it struggled to operate through the thick fog of Tokyo Bay. Ten explosions could be heard in the distance—that left five missiles unaccounted for.

The first missile struck the ship's primary communication mast, ripping it apart in a fiery explosion. A second and third soon followed, targeting the ship's front and rear radar systems. In a matter of moments, the Tiger Claw was rendered deaf and mute, its ability to communicate with the outside world obliterated.

Captain Lee and Admiral Chen were both knocked to the floor by the impact. Captain Lee looked around in disbelief. "What just happened?" he gasped, trying to comprehend the extent of the damage. Outside the bridge he saw his ship in flames, and the ship's alarm system indicated it was taking on water.

Admiral Chen snapped at Captain Lee. "Send men below deck to stop the flooding, ask Beijing for reinforce —"

The fourth missile struck the bridge with the force of a meteor, the explosion engulfing the structure in a blinding inferno. Admiral Chen and Captain Lee, caught in the epicenter of the blast, had no chance for escape. In an instant, they were vaporized in a firestorm hot enough to melt steel. The bridge, once the nerve center of the

Tiger Claw, was now an unrecognizable ruin, a gaping wound of molten metal and soot.

Before the crew of the ship could even process what happened, the final missile delivered the coup de grâce to the bridge. This second explosion decimated what little remained, totally decapitating the ship.

In the aftermath, the *Tiger Claw* was left reeling, a shadow of its former self. The command hierarchy was decimated, plunging the survivors into a mire of confusion and despair. Without their leaders and with critical systems destroyed, the crew scrambled to maintain what little control they had over the sinking ship. *Tiger Claw* was finished.

Back on the *Pasadena,* the crew stood at high alert. Their weapons launch had made enough noise for half of the Pacific Ocean to hear them. "*Sea Dragon* and every other Chinese submarine within 200 miles will be coming for us," said Captain Reese. "Maintain flank speed, and deploy countermeasures!"

The XO acknowledged and began executing the order. *Pasadena's* rear torpedo tube opened and ejected two barrel-shaped countermeasures. Each countermeasure emitted sounds to mimic the *Pasadena,* and electromagnetic emitters simulated the profile of a large metal submarine. This countermeasure gave up the *Pasadena's* location, but it created enough signal to cover their escape and attract any ordinance headed their way. Hopefully the four X-48s in sentinel mode would provide enough cover for them to get away from their launch position.

Tiger Claw sinks in Tokyo Bay.

10

Yokohama

Marvin checked his watch. It felt like hours, but only 10 minutes had gone by. He remembered Grace was bleeding out down below, and not 15 minutes ago he had just killed a man with his bare hands. Thoughts flooded his mind, but he had to focus—he had to watch for the launch signal. He had programmed the tower's radar system set to notify him of any weapons activity off the coast of Japan.

Suddenly a red alert popped on screen, notifying him of 16 missile launches. Pasadena had launched its payload against *Tiger Claw*!

Marvin didn't miss a beat. With *Tiger Claw's* communications system about to be destroyed, Marvin knew he had a brief window to exploit. He quickly initiated the fake transmission to *Sea Dragon:*

```
TIGER CLAW TO SEA DRAGON: Ambush from Japanese
submarine off the coast. You are ordered to seek
and destroy the enemy submarine. If under threat of
capture, do not fall into the hands of the enemy.
```

```
Provide current coordinates for attack
coordination.
```

The message was concise, manipulating the AI submarine's prime directive. Moments later, an acknowledgment message came back, and he decrypted *Sea Dragon's* coordinates. Marvin wasted no time and grabbed his satellite phone. He dialed a Japanese phone number.

"Captain Tanaka, this is Marvin Wong calling from the Crow's Nest," Marvin said. "I'm sending you the coordinates of *Sea Dragon*, accurate as of 10 seconds ago."

Captain Tanaka stood in the bridge of the JS *Yari*, just 10 miles off the coast of Tokyo. Captain Tanaka listened intently, his face set in grim determination. "Understood. We'll handle it."

"Also, I need to ask a favor," Marvin said.

"What do you need?"

"Send a medevac to my location. We have a lot of wounded soldiers here."

"We'll send it. Good luck."

The deafening roar of rotor blades filled the air as Japanese attack helicopters combed the mouth of Tokyo Bay. In a few minutes they hovered over *Sea Dragon's* last known location and dropped sonar buoys into the water, the electronic pings piercing the silent depths below. Some helicopters, equipped with electromagnetic sensors, hovered over the sea and scanned for blips in electromagnetic energy. The seascape was transformed into a pulsating grid, with sonar and electromagnetic imaging combining to isolate the *Sea Dragon's* exact position.

Tanaka observed the operations through camera feeds from the helicopters. As the data streams poured in, he saw *Sea Dragon's* position projected on to the 3D holo-map in the center of the bridge.

"Broadcast the coordinates to the gunships!" Tanaka commanded.

A nearby helicopter gunship, armed and ready, received the coordinates. Expertly programming its torpedo arsenal, it dropped four torpedoes into the water, their silver forms slicing through the waves, descending towards *Sea Dragon.*

Inside *Sea Dragon*, the AI's algorithms worked feverishly. It deployed countermeasures, released decoy signatures, and attempted defensive maneuvers. But the relentless barrage of torpedoes was overwhelming. Dozens of them, all zeroing in, their sonar locked onto the submarine with active guidance from the gunships' surface sonar and electromagnetic sensors. There was no escape.

Realizing the inevitable, *Sea Dragon* made a desperate last move. She began a rapid descent, the darkness of the abyss enveloping it. The pressure increased as it descended to 3,000 meters... 3,500 meters... It was getting close to its crush depth. The computer knew the odds – it was impossible to survive.

The first torpedo was 20 seconds away from impact. *Sea Dragon* initiated its self-destruct timer and calculated a firing solution to *Pasadena's* last known location. She opened her torpedo tubes and fired off a salvo of four Yu-7 torpedoes as a final parting gift.

The ocean depths, typically a world of muted sounds, were shattered by a colossal explosion. The shockwave rippled outwards, sending an aquatic shockwave that could be felt for miles. *Sea Dragon* was gone.

Above the water's surface, the violent eruption sent a massive plume of water skyward. The helicopters maneuvered away under a shower of saltwater.

Captain Tanaka breathed a sigh of relief. The *Sea Dragon* was dead.

Tanaka picked up the phone and called central command. "*Tiger Claw* and *Sea Dragon* are dead. Proceed with Phase 2."

Sea Dragon initiates its self-destruct sequence.

11

Pasadena had fled the scene at flank speed, and within 10 minutes traveled five nautical miles east of their initial launch position. She heard massive explosions near Tokyo Bay.

"Captain," said Ensign Clarke. "During our escape we detected two large explosions—one was *Tiger Claw* which sank after our barrage, and the other was most likely *Sea Dragon*. She detonated very deep, probably due to the torpedo barrage from Japanese anti-submarine forces."

Captain Reese picked up a receiver and broadcasted an update to the whole ship. "This is the captain. We have confirmed *Tiger Claw* and *Sea Dragon* are dead. Thank you all for your hard work."

The ship erupted in cheers and applause.

"XO, clear our baffles and take us home to Pearl Harbor," said Reese. "We need to re-arm after that Harpoon-X barrage."

"Aye, Captain," replied XO Smith. Smith initiated the order to turn the submarine and check the area behind it for sounds.

"Wait, Captain!" Ensign Clarke's exclamation pierced through the joyous atmosphere. "I'm detecting... four incoming Yu-7 torpedoes! They've evaded our countermeasures and are heading towards our direction at approximately 50 knots. Five minutes to impact!"

"What? How did we miss them?" asked Reese.

"The explosions had masked the sound of their launch, and we couldn't hear very well while traveling at flank. They might have been tailing us for miles, we didn't have time to clear the baffles."

Captain Reese's heart raced as he absorbed the news. "Battle stations! All hands, brace for evasive maneuvers!" he commanded.

The crew snapped into action, well-trained hands moving with precision and urgency. Clarke started analyzing the incoming threats.

"XO, prepare countermeasures," Reese ordered. "Deploy decoys and initiate evasive pattern Sierra-2."

"Aye, Captain," XO Smith replied, his fingers flying over the controls. "Decoys away!"

The *Pasadena* released countermeasures. As the decoys dispersed, the submarine sharply altered its course, diving deeper and banking to port in an attempt to throw off the pursuing torpedoes.

"Status on the torpedoes?" Reese asked.

"They're still tracking us, sir," Thompson replied. "Two have diverted towards the decoys, but two are adjusting to match our turn."

"Initiate countermeasure package Alpha," Reese commanded. "Launch everything we've got."

Pasadena emptied its supply of countermeasures, leaving behind a trail of 5 noisemaking, electromagnetic decoys. Without any additional countermeasures, *Pasadena* was running out of options.

"Coming about, hard starboard!" Reese ordered. The submarine banked sharply again.

"The two torpedoes are closing in, Captain," Thompson reported. "Three minutes to impact."

"Emergency blow!" Reese barked. "Surface the ship, now!"

The command sent the crew into a flurry of coordinated activity. High-pressure air blasted into the ballast tanks, forcing water out and causing the *Pasadena* to rise rapidly. The submarine rocketed towards the surface, its hull groaning under the strain.

"Prepare for impact!" Reese shouted, gripping the edge of his chair as the *Pasadena* broke the surface with a thunderous roar.

One of the torpedoes struck one of the decoys and detonated, sending a violent shockwave through the water. The second torpedo, however, was not so easily deceived. It closed in rapidly, detonating in the water near the *Pasadena's* aft compartment just as the submarine breached the surface. The explosion was deafening, and the force of it sent a shudder through the entire vessel. The shockwave tossed Reese off his feet.

"Damage report!" Reese demanded, as alarms blared and the crew scrambled to assess the situation.

"We've got a breach in the aft compartment, Captain!" Smith yelled. "Flooding reported in sections three and four!"

"Seal it off, now!" Reese ordered. "Damage control teams to the aft compartment!"

The crew worked swiftly, sealing bulkheads and deploying pumps to control the flooding. Despite the chaos, their training and discipline shone through. The breach was contained, but not without significant effort and the loss of some precious equipment.

"Status?" Reese asked, as the crew began to regain control of the situation.

"We've stopped the flooding, sir," Smith reported, panting. "But we've taken damage. One of our thrusters was destroyed, but we can limp back to Pearl Harbor. We also can't submerge."

Reese nodded, relief mingled with exhaustion on his face. "Do we have any assets in the area that we can link up with?"

"Aye sir, there is a carrier group about 400 miles south of us near the Philippine Sea," replied Smith.

"Send a message to them. Ask if they can send a destroyer escort to help get us to Hawaii. If we can't submerge, we're sitting ducks out here."

The *Pasadena* headed east towards Hawaii, its engines struggling but functional. The crew settled into the long journey home, their spirits buoyed by their survival and the knowledge that they had struck a significant blow against their adversaries.

12

Somewhere over the Yellow Sea

Captain Emori's heart raced as he approached the final leg of his journey. The silence of the cockpit was a stark contrast to the turmoil within. He had just crossed into Chinese airspace.

Captain Emori looked at the clock on the display of his F-X hypersonic bomber, the *Yamato*. He was on time. He had been flying from Sapporo, southwest across South Korea and over the Yellow Sea. The display showed his current altitude and speed: Mach 8 at 30,000 meters. The F-X bomber was Japan's secret project, blessed with next-generation stealth and hypersonic propulsion which surpassed that of the United States' SR-72 Darkstar. The *Yamato* possessed special radar-absorbing nanotechnology, giving it the radar cross-section of a pigeon. It could sustain extremely high speeds at high altitude thanks to its hybrid scramjet engines and heat resistant armor. Recessed engines made it difficult to detect with infrared sensors from the ground or space. Today, *Yamato* carried a special payload of eight long-range anti-ground hypersonic glide missiles (LRAGHMs), each equipped with stealth technology and a 500 kilogram bunker-busting warhead that could penetrate 10 meters into reinforced concrete before detonation.

Emori's approach was calculated, the route meticulously planned to avoid detection and interception. The F-X's advanced technology had served him well, rendering him invisible to the prying eyes of radar or satellite systems.

He began his descent as he approached Hubei Province, approximately 300 kilometers from the target. At an altitude of 24,000 meters he opened the bay doors and released his payload. Each LRAGHM fell to earth for a few seconds and ignited its two-stage engine. Each missile behaved like a small aircraft, complete with a scramjet engine, wings, and steering capability. An onboard neural chip optimized the missile path to avoid known radar sites or anti-aircraft installations, and each missile eventually settled into a low-altitude approach velocity of Mach 0.9. As it approached subsonic speed, the LRAGHM switched to turbofan-mode to maintain a stealthy approach for the last 10 kilometers of its flight. Each LRAGHM skimmed the surface of the earth, using computer vision to easily steer around tall buildings or trees. At such a low altitude, they easily avoided radar detection.

Emori slowed to Mach 5 and began his descent. His target lay in the heart of China, an imposing monolith of concrete and steel standing silently against the night. The Three Gorges Dam, a marvel of human engineering, loomed large in the darkness, its vast expanse stretching across the Yangtze River. Moonlight glinted off its smooth, gray surface, casting long, ethereal shadows that danced on the water below. The dam, formidable and serene, embodied the power of human ingenuity and the raw force of nature, working in harmonious concert to produce 22.5 gigawatts of power for an energy-hungry populace.

It was midnight. The dam exuded an aura of tranquility. The usual bustle of daytime operations had quieted, leaving only the soft, rhythmic hum of turbines spinning deep within its core. From a distance, the sound of water flowing through the spillways was a constant, calming rush, like a great heartbeat in the stillness of the night. The mighty Yangtze, tamed yet persistent, flowed steadily, its surface reflecting the twinkling stars above.

The dam was now just 150 kilometers away. Emori continued his descent and switched his hybrid engine into ramjet mode for supercruise flight at Mach 3. His hands were steady on the controls as he reduced altitude.

At this moment, Emori's LRAGHMS found their targets. Four missiles hit radar outposts along his approach vector, clearing a path to the dam. The remaining four missiles skimmed the Yangtze just a few meters above the surface and careened towards Three Gorges Dam. The first LRAGHM pierced 10 meters into the dam's center just above the water line, blasting a huge hole. The second missile hit the same location on the dam and blasted an even deeper hole. The explosions echoed through the valley, a prelude to the devastation that was to come. But the concrete held strong. Together, the four LRAGHMs drilled a tunnel into the dam approximately 60 meters deep and 20 meters wide. The missiles weren't designed to destroy the dam—only to prime it. Three Gorges Dam was over 100 meters thick, so small bombs would not break it. But a well-placed 60-meter deep bore hole, just wide enough for *Yamato* to fly through, could be used to deliver a large explosive to the core of the dam.

Alarms at the Three Gorges Dam control center immediately alerted nearby PLA forces that something was happening. The PLA Air Force redirected fighters in the area, but it would take them a few minutes to arrive. Emori accelerated to Mach 5 as he flew past the city of Yichang. At that speed, his heat signature would ruin his stealth, but that wasn't important anymore. It was a straight shot to the dam now, and at Mach 5 he could cover the remaining 50 kilometers to the target in less than 30 seconds. The outside of the *Yamato* was red hot from air friction.

Yamato began to superheat, but its heat resistant polymer provided some protection. A plasma sheath formed around the plane as well, eliminating all radio communications. China had developed anti-aircraft laser weapons and deployed them in the mountains around Three Gorges Dam. Multiple lasers locked on to Emori and dumped beam energy into his aircraft, attempting to melt him out of the sky. The plasma sheath, however, rendered these heat lasers totally ineffective—deflecting the heat energy and allowing Emori to speed through unscathed. The PLA's anti-aircraft laser system was completely useless against the hypersonic *Yamato*. Emori instructed *Yamato's* neural processor to take over flight controls and execute the final approach. Emori unbuckled from his seat and headed to the rear of the ship for the last part of his mission. Twenty seconds remained.

Captain Emori's kneeled over a large metal box with a spherical core extending out the top. This was *Yamato's* final gift—10,000 kilograms of next-generation explosive which delivered the equivalent of 35,000 pounds of TNT when detonated. All he had to do was enter the four-digit arming code code, and the ship's onboard computer would synchronize the bomb detonation to maximize damage to the center of the dam. Emori punched in the code. The display panel flashed the word "ARMED".

With the neural engine piloting the ship and the bomb now fully armed, Emori had nothing left to do. Ten seconds remained.

He couldn't forget the images of Osaka, now a smoldering ruin after China's attack. The cries of millions of Japanese lives lost echoed in his mind. The destruction, the senseless devastation, all inflicted by the very nation he was now hurtling towards. A wave of sorrow and anger washed over him. This mission was more than just a strike; it was retribution. The CCP would pay for their sins.

Emori sat next to the bomb and thought about his life. His thoughts turned to his parents. He could see their faces, etched with worry and love. Would they understand? Would they forgive him for this ultimate sacrifice? He hoped so. He hoped they would see the honor in his actions, the necessity of his choice to give his life for the country he loved. The countdown flashed on the bomb's display: 5… 4… 3… 2… 1…

In those fleeting moments, Captain Emori found a strange peace. He was avenging Osaka, honoring his homeland, and ensuring a safer future for Japan.

"Nihon Banzai!" Screamed Emori. Long live Japan!

Yamato sailed right into the freshly carved tunnel on the side of Three Gorges Dam. Its neural processor calculated the exact instant to detonate its payload to deliver maximum damage to the concrete superstructure.

The explosion was monumental, tearing completely through the back wall of the dam and unleashing a torrent of water. The river, once tamed by the dam, reclaimed its dominion with a vengeance, ripping through and dislodging car-sized concrete blocks from the superstructure. The dam crumbled, unleashing a 100 meter wave downstream towards unsuspecting cities, villages, and farmland.

The wavefront traveled at 100 kilometers per hour. It tore into buildings, tossed cars off roads like playthings, and drowned everything in its path. The torrent reshaped the landscape and enveloped cities. Drowning deaths surpassed 10 million overnight. Japan had inflicted a death toll equivalent to erasing Beijing and Shanghai off the map. At no point in human history had so many people died so quickly.

Satellite imagery

Lat: 30.8233, Long: 111.0037

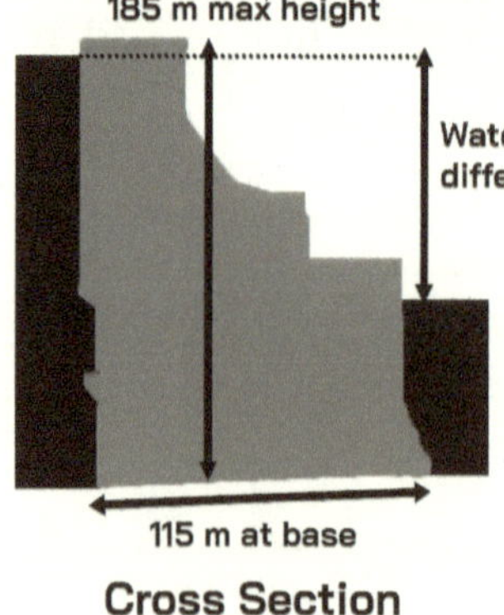

Three Gorges Dam

Key Information
Construction began: 1994
First operational: 2009
Total concrete: 28M cubic meters
Max power putput: 22.5 gigawatts

Captain Emori arms the 10,000 kilogram explosive.

13

The Presidential Compound in Beijing

Zheng Song Han sat alone in silence. The Three Gorges Dam, a symbol of China's engineering might and economic prosperity, had been attacked, leading to a catastrophe larger than anything the country had experienced before.

He read the report twice, not because the words were confusing, but because his mind refused to accept the reality they conveyed. Over 10 million dead, hundreds of millions displaced, and an impending famine that could claim untold millions of lives in the coming months. Wuhan, almost 380 kilometers away from the remnants of Three Gorges Dam, sat under seven meters of water. Then there was the destruction of *Tiger Claw* and *Sea Dragon*, and the loss of his dear friend Chen Yi cutting even deeper. Chen's death symbolized the end of an era, the loss of not just a friend but of a vision for China that now lay in ruins. Zheng Song Han, who never married nor had any children of his own, was alone. And his grip on China—the only thing he truly ever loved—was slipping fast.

As he sat there, the weight of his decisions pressed upon him. His Secretary of Defense, Ming Di, had come seeking guidance, hoping for a plan to retaliate, to show strength. But Zheng knew better. Retaliation would only lead to further destruction, an endless cycle of violence that would bleed China dry. This strike on the Three Gorges Dam was a crippling blow. His dream of a united Asia, leading the world into a new era, crumbled to dust in his hands.

Zheng saw the writing on the wall. China strikes back, Japan strikes back, ad infinitum. Meanwhile there would be riots in the streets of China as famine and anarchy reigned… His attempt to pull Japan into a China-led defensive alliance had failed, and further attempts would result in unacceptable losses on both sides.

"You don't understand, Ming. This attack hit a critical artery in China and we are no longer in the position to wage a global war. One-third of our population is without electricity. How can we unite the Pacific when anarchy and chaos are just a few days away? Our people will devolve into barbarism if we don't fix our problems at home."

"So what now?" Ming asked. "We just sit and take it?"

"China must heal. We must bide our time, but we will most certainly return and make them pay. Don't worry Ming, we must strike when we are strong, not when we are weak."

Zheng felt empty. His refusal to act was not borne out of cowardice, but out of a realization that any further aggression would only exacerbate the suffering of his people. But how could he convey the depth of this realization to Ming, to anyone, when all around them, their world was collapsing?

Zheng clenched his fist on his desk and hunched over. He had been so close to uniting Asia. Like Icarus, he had flown too close to the sun and lost his wings. Over 400 million people would starve in the next 30 days. He had failed his people.

Ming turned and left quickly. Zheng could see the loss of trust in Ming's eyes—perhaps Ming would stage a coup one day. But that wasn't important right now. Zheng opened his desk drawer and reached for his bottle of baijiu, a distilled whiskey made in his hometown. It wasn't the best alcohol available, but it reminded him of his youthful ideals and the countryside.

Zheng poured himself a shot and gulped it down. He saw the alerts coming through on his computer—the encrypted messages from his military commanders, the new clippings shared from his press team. His phone rang constantly. His entire legacy was dissolving before his very eyes. He knew he needed to lead his people out of this dark time, but how could he do this when he was responsible for their suffering in the first place?

He grabbed some stationery and scribbled out a note. He felt the baijiu hitting his bloodstream, the slight numbness offering a little solace from the emptiness inside.

He reached farther into the drawer and felt the cold grip of his 9mm handgun. He kept it loaded and ready in case of an assassination attempt.

He pulled the slide back to check for a round in the chamber. He could barely comprehend the number of lives lost. He had failed China miserably. Perhaps his final act might serve as a catalyst for change, a wake-up call to those who would follow to lead with compassion, to break the cycle of violence and retaliation, and to rebuild the nation he loved from the ashes of its darkest hour. Or maybe it would have the opposite effect and enrage his country to global war? Would the CCP survive? Whatever happened next, it wasn't his concern anymore. Zheng closed his eyes and wrapped his lips around the barrel of the gun.

The sound of the gunshot echoed through the empty office, a lone punctuation mark in the silence that followed. Zheng Song Han, Paramount Leader of China and General Secretary of the Chinese Communist Party, was gone. The impact of his life, his decisions, and his death would reverberate through the annals of history, a tragic reminder of the cost of ambition and the fragility of power.

Aftermath of the retaliatory strike on Three Gorges Dam.

Part Seven

Epilogue

1

Woodlawn Cemetery in Colma, California

It was raining, the sky was a blanket of leaden clouds that mourned the day. Marvin stood fifty yards away from the throng of people adorned in black, their umbrellas like dark flowers in the rain. The drone of eulogies and soft sobs was swallowed by the steady drumming of rain on canvas and earth. Marvin, enveloped in his solitude, watched from afar as the teary-eyed relatives of the deceased grieved.

As the ceremony dwindled and people dispersed, Marvin approached the freshly installed grave with solemn steps, his umbrella shielding him from the rain. The world around him seemed to mute, leaving only the pitter-patter of raindrops and the sound of his wet footsteps as a somber soundtrack. He knelt before the grave and read the inscription:

GRACE KIM
May 17, 2029 - December 15, 2058
A loving daughter and friend.

The family, who did not know Grace was in the CIA, was told she died in a car accident while traveling overseas. Memories flooded Marvin's mind, vivid like a dream. He remembered holding Grace in his arms, her lifeblood ebbing away. Could he have saved her?

"Did you know her?" The inquiry, soft and laden with grief, came from a man standing behind Marvin. Startled, Marvin turned to find an elderly Asian couple huddled under an umbrella, their eyes hung low.

"Yes, I knew her from… college," Marvin lied, the words tasting like ash on his tongue. It was a necessary deception, a shield to protect them from the harrowing truth of their daughter's clandestine life.

"Oh, you went to UC Berkeley too?" the woman sobbed. "We had no idea Grace still had friends in the area. Her Berkeley days were so long ago, after all."

Marvin introduced himself. He learned that the couple was Grace's parents. He ached to share the magnitude of their daughter's bravery—to recount the tales of how she had recruited him into the CIA, her genius that led them through impossible missions, and ultimately, her selfless act that saved countless lives from the brink of destruction.

Grace's father gave his wife a hug.

"Thank you for coming Marvin, it was nice to meet you," Grace's mother whispered through her sobs. Marvin nodded, his heart heavy with the stories untold, the heroism unacknowledged. As he stood and walked away, the rain seemed to wash over him, a cleansing torrent that could not cleanse his soul of the memories, the loss, and the unyielding respect for Grace Kim—a hero laid to rest.

2

Two months later

The familiar gray fog of San Francisco hovered above the streets, casting a dreamy shroud over the city. But it couldn't match the haze that enveloped Marvin's mind. Here he was, back in his small apartment. The CIA had gifted him an anonymous wallet filled with 100 million FedCoins. It was a sum that made him, in an instant, one of the city's nouveau riche. Yet, as he scrolled through messages on his MetaMind headset, he realized some things hadn't changed at all.

"I had an amazing time," read the message from yesterday's date. "But I just didn't feel the connection."

Marvin sighed and took off his MetaMind. Another one bites the dust. It seemed like all the girls in the Bay Area had problems feeling the "connection" with him. Maybe it was because they sensed he was hiding something—the shadows of his past missions, the weight of secrets, the world-altering decisions. He couldn't reveal any of his work or his newfound wealth. To these San

Francisco girls, he was just another Asian software engineer.

But maybe it wasn't the right time for him to date anyone. Grace's funeral had been a difficult time for him. He hadn't realized it before, but he developed feelings for her. All those evenings connecting over drinks at the jazz club in San Francisco, those hours spent working together at Langley… He had started to grow fond of her big attitude and sarcastic humor. She projected a strong image and kept people on their toes, but Marvin had come to know her as a beautiful and talented woman with a bright future ahead of her.

The CIA gave him six months of leave to recover from the mission. He knew he could return to the CIA if he wanted to, or he could resign and move on. The thought of returning to the CIA without Grace felt wrong.

He had conquered the digital realms, outsmarted adversaries in shadows, and emerged victorious where many had faltered. Yet, the victory felt hollow. His money and his technical accolades offered no warmth, no companionship.

Marvin's MetaMind beeped. He put it on and saw a pop-up notification: "Golden Rat has invited you to play Medieval Swords!"

Golden Rat? What could he want? He joined the game and was immediately transported to a familiar, grassy battlefield. He looked around and saw Golden Rat, a tall burly knight wielding a giant axe. Golden Rat swung at him, and he defended with his shield and sword. After a few rounds of play, Marvin tossed his sword aside.

"What do you want, Golden Rat?" Marvin asked, using his voice modulator.

"Hi Titanium," Golden Rat replied with a similar anonymized voice. "How's it going?"

"Just been laying low. That intel you gave us was excellent, by the way. I'm not sure where you get your information from, but keep it coming."

"There are a lot of things you need to know. What you've done and seen is just the tip of the iceberg. We should meet in person."

"You sure you want to do that? I'm CIA, and I thought you wanted to stay anonymous."

"I think I can trust you after seeing what you did with my information. Just come to these coordinates, and tell no one you're coming."

Golden Rat sent the coordinates: -16.981302, 177.367518.

Marvin plugged the coordinates into his map tool. It was a spot in the ocean amidst a chain of Fijian islands. The kind of place you go to relax—not exactly a place for a clandestine meeting.

The game exited. "Golden Rat has signed off," spoke the in-game announcer. Marvin opened a taxi application and requested a self-driving car to San Francisco International Spaceport. He tossed the MetaMind into his suitcase, along with a few days' worth of clothes, and opened his apartment door to leave. He took one last look at his old San Francisco apartment. He had a feeling he wouldn't be back for a while. He sighed, and with a slight grin, closed the door and stepped outside to find his taxi.

The sleek black vehicle pulled up by the curb and he climbed aboard. "Would you like a drink, sir?" asked an onboard AI.

"Sure, mix me something tropical," Marvin said.

After a few beeps and some buzzing sounds, the glove compartment opened up with a full cocktail glass inside. He grabbed it and gave it a sip. “I might as well enjoy the trip to Fiji,” he thought.

Marvin dialed a private charter service at the spaceport. “Yes sir, how can I help you?” asked the AI agent on the other end.

“I need a private flight to Fiji,” Marvin said. “What are my options?”

“We can get you to Fiji in comfort, sir. If you are chartering a private aircraft, we can offer you hypersonic travel and get you to Fiji in two hours. Would you like to book this flight for 30,000 FedCoins?”

“Sure, book it for me. Send me the secure payment link. I’ll be at the Spaceport in 30 minutes.”

Marvin received a payment request on his phone. He wired over 30,000 FedCoins and wondered what Fiji had in store for him.

3

Marvin's driverless taxi weaved through the streets of San Francisco, its silent, electric engine humming as it navigated towards San Francisco International Spaceport. The city, aglow with holographic advertisements that faded in and out of the fog, felt surreal and abandoned at this late hour. Marvin's taxi would bypass the public entrance of the spaceport and take him directly to the hangar for private charters.

He disembarked from the taxi, which softly chimed a farewell before disappearing into the dark of night. Marvin approached his sleek hypersonic aircraft housed within the hangar, its body gleaming under the soft glow of LED lights. The hangar itself was a marvel of modern architecture, with transparent solar panels doubling as the roof, and walls lined with reactive screens that displayed serene landscapes to calm travelers before their journeys.

The aircraft's design was the epitome of futuristic engineering, its contours sharp and promising unparalleled speed. Entirely unmanned, the craft was equipped with an AI concierge that greeted Marvin warmly as he boarded. "Welcome, Mr. Wong. Your hypersonic journey to Fiji will be approximately two hours. Please, make yourself comfortable," the AI's soothing voice informed him, emanating from hidden speakers.

Inside, the cabin was tailored to luxurious perfection. Seats with memory foam adjusted dynamically to his body shape, offering an almost weightless feeling. Gourmet food, prepared by robotic systems capable of mimicking the techniques of top chefs, and a selection of fine beverages chilled to precise temperatures, were readily available. The entertainment system offered an array of virtual reality experiences, interactive games, and a library of both classic and contemporary films streamed directly to personal viewing screens. He also had access to terabit Internet speeds at any altitude.

As the engines began their quiet hum, vibrating slightly as they prepared to defy the bounds of speed, Marvin settled into his seat. He reclined the chair, feeling it adjust to his body with comforting precision. Pulling out his phone, he quickly secured a private, autonomous catamaran from Nadi International Spaceport in Fiji; his resources now allowed for no less than the utmost discretion and comfort.

The aircraft soon lifted off, soaring into the night sky. Below him, the lights of San Francisco merged into a tapestry of darkness and twinkling city lights, gradually giving way to the black expanse of the Pacific Ocean. From his window seat, Marvin watched the world transform, his thoughts drifting to the upcoming encounter. He pondered the scant details he knew about Golden Rat. What was the true nature of this secretive figure?

Leaning back, Marvin allowed himself to be lost in thought, the whisper of the aircraft's engines a comforting backdrop to his contemplations. He closed his eyes to rest. When he next opened them, he would be in Fiji, stepping into the next chapter of his quest.

4

Off the coast of Fiji

A lone 48-foot yacht floated lazily in the Fijian waters. The sun cast brilliant reflections across the ocean, illuminating the yacht's sleek design. It bobbed gently, the sound of water lapping against its hull blending with the distant cries of seagulls. A lithe figure emerged from the azure depths, a spear in hand, glistening with droplets and bearing the evening's catch. The swimmer approached the yacht, climbed aboard, and entered the rear doorway.

Marvin saw the yacht in the distance. Through binoculars, he scanned the vessel, noting the name "Golden Rat" elegantly scripted near a metallic emblem of a rat carrying a sword. "That has to be him," Marvin muttered under his breath, his pulse quickening with both excitement and trepidation.

He directed the catamaran closer to the yacht, skillfully maneuvering the controls as he approached. Once within a reasonable distance, he tossed a rope expertly onto the yacht's deck, securing the two vessels together. He stepped across the short gap between the ships, his heart pounding with anticipation. Tying off his catamaran, he moved towards the rear entrance of the ship.

The door was wide open. Inside, the yacht was outfitted like a comfortable living quarters, complete with a small kitchen and cozy seating area. The scent of fresh brewed mint tea blended with the salty sea air, creating an inviting atmosphere. Jazz played softly on the ship's sound system.

Marvin hesitated at the door, not sure whether to feel exhilarated or intimidated by what might await him inside. He took a deep breath and stepped into the boat, his eyes scanning the interior.

His gaze landed on a striking figure reclining casually on a sofa draped in sunlight—Grace Kim! She wore a familiar emerald green bikini, looking serene and impossibly vibrant.

"It took you long enough!" Grace's voice broke through his shock, her tone light and teasing.

Marvin approached, speechless, his steps faltering as he took in her presence. She was supposed to be dead; he had mourned her. Yet here she was, beautiful as ever. Overcome by a torrent of emotions, he knelt down and wrapped his arms around her. They embraced.

Grace's laughter filled the cabin, warm and affectionate. "Just like old times, huh?" She squeezed his hand.

As Marvin withdrew slightly, his mind raced with questions. "Sorry, I just... How are you here? Am I dreaming? I saw you..." His voice trailed off, unable to articulate the memory of her lifeless body.

Grace sat up and looked seriously at Marvin. "The Japanese military took me to the hospital in critical condition. I died for an hour. But their technology is decades ahead of ours. They used nanotechnology and stem cells to revive my brain. They synthesized a new stomach and liver for me, along with a gallon of synthetic blood."

Marvin was shocked. "What about the SEALs? Were they saved?"

Grace shook her head somberly. "Unfortunately, they weren't so lucky. They had been critically wounded, beyond the help of even the most advanced medical interventions. They died long before the medevac arrived. And even Japan's cutting-edge medical technology has its limitations. If the medevac had been delayed by even ten minutes, I probably would have died with the SEALs."

Marvin took a deep breath, trying to process the enormity of what she was saying. "I can't believe it," he murmured, his voice thick with emotion. "I was there at your funeral, Grace. I mourned you."

"I'm sorry you had to go through that, Marvin. The CIA thought it was best that I remain dead to the world. Technically, I'm not even supposed to be talking to you right now, but I don't care anymore. Dying changes your perspective on life." Grace's voice was a mix of resignation and newfound clarity.

Marvin looked at her, confusion etched across his face. "There's one thing that I can't figure out," he said, his brow furrowed. "How are you Golden Rat? Why all the subterfuge to get information that you already knew?"

Grace leaned forward, her gaze intense. "We needed to be absolutely sure we could trust you," she explained. "You didn't disappoint. You made contact with the informant, gathered the necessary information, and managed all of it without raising any suspicion. Golden

Rat is more than just an alias—it's an international identity I use to source intelligence. It's an alias that lets me stay in the shadows, still connected with my contacts across the dark web."

"So, what now, Grace?" Marvin asked, a hopeful note in his voice as he looked towards a future that seemed suddenly wide open.

"Well, I'm officially dead, and you're on paid leave. I think we're due for a little downtime. A vacation to really unwind and process all of this."

Marvin's face broke into a smile, a genuine one that reached his eyes. "That sounds perfect. Where do you have in mind?"

"Bali's wonderful this time of year," Grace replied, her eyes lighting up with the prospect of new adventures.

The sun began to dip below the horizon, casting a golden glow that bathed the yacht in warm light. Marvin stood up, offering his hand to Grace. She took it with a smile that seemed to promise more than just a new destination. Hand in hand, they walked towards the inner cabin, their steps light on the wooden deck.

Inside the cabin, Marvin turned to Grace, his eyes searching hers in the dimming light. The cabin door closed behind them with a soft click, sealing away the world. Inside, the space was cozy, illuminated by the soft glow of lamps casting gentle shadows across the wood-paneled interior.

Grace's gaze lingered on Marvin, seeing him not as the timid software engineer she had first met in the bustling streets of San Francisco, but as a man transformed. The trials they had endured together had reshaped him into a warrior. His confidence now was a steady presence that filled the room. The Marvin who had once doubted his place in the world had shed that uncertainty and stood before her as an entirely different animal.

"Grace," Marvin whispered, his voice a velvety caress that sent shivers down her spine. He drew closer, staring deep into her eyes.

Marvin brushed his lips against hers, soft and tentative at first. Grace's response was immediate. Her hands rose to his face, fingers trembling slightly as they traced the contours of his jawline, pulling him deeper into the kiss. Her other hand pressed against his chest, feeling the rapid beat of his heart. Grace's hand moved from his face, sliding into his hair, tugging him closer, her actions a silent plea for closeness that no words could express. Marvin's arms encircled her waist, drawing her body against his.

The duo had been to hell and back, and in the process prevented an authoritarian regime from conquering the Asia Pacific. The world was safe, but for how long? While the world searched for answers, our heroes enjoyed a much deserved break from the action. Aboard *Golden Rat,* in the tropical waters of Fiji, the world's problems felt just a little less urgent.

Marvin and Grace head to their next adventure.

QUANTUM PERIL

6c978976619af79a6bf5fa3b391cc3b5

Nolan Lee

Afterward

My father's family immigrated to the USA in the early 1900s to build a better life. Meanwhile, my mother's family immigrated around the 1960s after living through the failures of Maoist China and the Great Leap Forward. Both sides of my family come from Guangdong, one of the Kuomintang's last footholds in China before the Chinese Communist Party (CCP) completely seized the mainland. Many of today's immigrant Chinese have mysterious wealth from the mainland—they come to America to buy up properties or pay out-of-state tuition to pursue degrees at our universities. Not my family, however. We came to America with little, and through hard work and frugality we earned our way into the middle class.

On my father's side, we had an opportunity to contribute to America's defense. Many of my grand uncles enlisted to fight in America's wars. My grandfather, an army technician, met my grandmother in the service. Congress recently recognized Chinese American veterans of WWII with a Congressional Gold Medal, and my family proudly displays a replica of the medal in honor of my ancestors. In a life of conflict and political differences, we must pick a side. And my family has firmly sided with America. We are thankful to this country for providing us with a new chance at life. While the United States has a history of cruelty and racism against Chinese people, the overall trend is positive and we still feel like we are welcome here.

When I wrote this book, I wanted to tell a story inspired by current events and investigate what could happen if the United States fell behind an ever more aggressive CCP-led China. I wanted explore the threat that the CCP poses to the world, but I also wanted to do this without casting ethnic Chinese in a xenophobic light.

When discussing China, it is important to separate the Chinese people from the CCP. The CCP is an authoritarian regime. While political parties still exist in China, they exist at the pleasure of the CCP and do not operate as opposition parties. These parties simply provide the CCP with feedback and suggestions about policy issues, and effectively have no power to run the country. In China, the role of President is largely symbolic and is usually held by the General Secretary of the CCP. To make matters more confusing, the Paramount Leader of China is superior to the President and General Secretary. You can also hold the role of Chairman of the Central Military Commission (CMC) without holding any other roles—effectively making yourself the military dictator of the country. Deng Xiaoping used his role as Chairman of the CMC to reshape the CCP and propel himself to Paramount Leader despite never holding General Secretary or Presidential roles. Today all of these roles—Paramount Leader, General Secretary, President, and Chairman of the CMC are concentrated in one person: Xi Jinping.

These critical roles are not directly elected by the people of China. In the West, it is hard for us to comprehend that the leader of your country is selected through a closed-door. process. In America, we vote for our President. In China, voting is left to members of the CCP. The CCP holds a firm grip on the executive, judicial, and legislative bodies of government. Because the CCP is the only governing power in the People's Republic of China, I often use "China" and "CCP" interchangeably.

Most authoritarian regimes destroy themselves through human incompetence. The USSR bankrupted itself through central planning. Even the Kuomintang, which enjoyed absolute power in China prior to the rise of the CCP, was infected by corruption. The CCP studied the mistakes of past regimes to form their current system, much like our Founding Fathers who studied the mistakes of past democracies to design our Republic. The CCP has evolved into the strongest authoritarian regime on earth, and I do not believe it will collapse on its own.

The CCP leverages market economics to power its economic machine. It uses unchallenged domestic power to concentrate tax revenues into police and military forces that can quash any rebellion. The West had believed that market economics would encourage China to follow in the footsteps of Western democracies—but this was an error of judgement that the CCP exploited. The CCP gladly accepted wealth and technology from Western trade but continued to suppress free speech and the democratic process. It prevented its people from ever developing a voice that might challenge CCP rule, but rewarded them with food and housing and other material gifts.

China continues to enrich itself through one-sided access to Western markets. While the CCP has banned all American social media companies from operating within China, America allows Chinese apps to operate indiscriminately. We still allow apps like Weibo, WeChat, TikTok, and Xiaohongshu ("Little Red Book") to operate in our borders. These apps live in our phones and access our address books, our location information, our device information, and more. They greet our kids in the morning before they go to school, and they lull them to sleep at bedtime. Many Americans hesitate to ban TikTok because they make money on the app through advertising or sponsorships. The CCP is betting on our addiction to their apps to keep their money machine going. But we need to insist on reciprocal business—until businesses like Facebook, Instagram, or X (formerly Twitter) can operate in China, we must not allow TikTok or any China-owned app from operating in America. Their apps are digital trade routes for the CCP to pump content into our brains, mine our personal data, and make billions of dollars in the process.

The CCP also exerts shadow influence over any Chinese company operating within our borders. It is not a coincidence that the CCP has banned TikTok from operating within China, but it allows ByteDance to operate TikTok within the United States. The CCP understands the addictive nature of TikTok. It understands how these algorithms can manipulate young minds, and it protects its citizens from the platform.

Can the CCP be stopped? China's massive economy produces enough wealth to sustain the Party indefinitely, and as long as the military unquestioningly carries out the wishes of the Paramount Leader there will never be a military coup. The people of China largely avoid politics and would rather work hard, earn money, and live a peaceful life. Like it or not, the CCP is here to stay.

Once the CCP further develops AI, it may be able to leverage automation at unprecedented scale and exert massive influence over cyberspace. Military technology equipped with AI, much like in this novel, could level the playing field with the West. We must not underestimate the CCP's ability to innovate. It historically used copycat innovation to catch up to the United States, and China is at a juncture where it has enough talent and resources to create novel innovations that could surpass our own technology. And if it wants an update on our latest technology, it simply allows some of its smartest people to venture to the West. Why do you think so many Chinese PhD students and visa workers go to Apple, Microsoft, Nvidia, etc? The CCP doesn't need espionage to copy our technology. Their citizens, acting in their own self-interest, invariably bring American knowledge and expertise back to fuel the economic machine. In a peaceful, cooperative environment, all countries benefit from free trade of knowledge and resources. People bring wealth and knowledge back to their home countries, their countries develop and improve, and the world grows together. The CCP, however, co-opts wealth and innovation to become ever stronger in its fight against freedom and democracy.

When I visited China for the first time in 2007, I never imagined China's sudden rise as a superpower. Much of China still felt backwards then; public infrastructure was limited, medicine was limited, and much of the country was poor. But since the 2008 Olympics and the West's missteps after the Global Financial Crisis of 2007-2008 and the Pandemic of 2020, China has caught up.

With the CCP at the helm, China marches ever closer to global dominance. Every day, they advance while our leaders bicker and mismanage our economy. As we get bogged down in internal issues, the CCP marches ever closer to global supremacy. Unless the West pulls itself together, my novel might turn out to be more prophecy than fiction. For all our sakes, I hope it remains fiction.

Nolan Lee
Pasadena, California
August 10, 2024

Special Thanks

Thank you to all my friends and family who peer reviewed early editions of this book or supported me along the way. Without you, I would not have been able to bring this story to life!

A. A., A. H., R. H., K. S., S. C., J. B.

Mom, Dad, and Grandma.

I'd also like to thank my relatives who served the United States during WWII and subsequent wars. I hope to one day be as brave as you.

About the Author

Nolan Lee is a Chinese American author from Los Angeles, California. He studied engineering at the University of California, Berkeley, and received his master's degree in computer science from the Georgia Institute of Technology. Nolan's academic and professional backgrounds enable him to imbue his stories with a high level of scientific and technological accuracy.

Contact Information
Email: AuthorNolanLee@gmail.com
Instagram: @AuthorNolanLee

www.ingramcontent.com/pod-product-compliance
Lightning Source LLC
LaVergne TN
LVHW100520110826
845146LV00002B/716
* 9 7 9 8 9 9 0 7 9 9 7 1 4 *